Marian Brewster

Under the Water-Oaks

Marian Brewster

Under the Water-Oaks

ISBN/EAN: 9783742812605

Manufactured in Europe, USA, Canada, Australia, Japa

Cover: Foto ©Andreas Hilbeck / pixelio.de

Manufactured and distributed by brebook publishing software
(www.brebook.com)

Marian Brewster

Under the Water-Oaks

UNDER THE WATER-OAKS

BY

MARIAN BREWSTER

ILLUSTRATED BY J. F. GOODRIDGE

BOSTON
ROBERTS BROTHERS
1892

University Press:
JOHN WILSON AND SON, CAMBRIDGE, U.S.A.

CONTENTS.

UNDER THE WATER-OAKS.

CHAPTER I.

HOW NAP WAS NIPPED.

" Hum-mum-mum ; hum-mum-mum," buzzed the bees all day in the top of the water-oaks.

" Hum-mum-mum," hummed Nap down below, for he knew what secret the bees were keeping so mum about.

The little darky was lying on the broad gallery of the house that nestles under the water-oaks, kicking up his bare heels and eating a sweet potato.

Brer and Gene also were eating sweet potatoes. The three boys always were engaged in this delectable pastime when there was nothing more exciting for them to do; unless, indeed, the supply of this cold refreshment had already been exhausted from Aunt Nance's kitchen-safe by their voracious appetites. Brer and Gene, however, had not keeled over in the easy attitude of their black play-fellow; they sat with more dignity on the gallery steps, their broad-brimmed hats pushed far back on their heads, and their elbows resting comfortably on their knees as they munched their sweet potatoes, and impartially tossed titbits of brown peeling to the dogs, who had gathered at the foot of the steps in an expectant but orderly circle, — for each dog was very well aware that if he wagged his tail too greedily, or spoke up before his turn, he would be ruthlessly passed by until the next round.

The two brothers were well-built, handsome little fellows, with intelligent well-bred faces such as one would hardly expect to see in the backwoods; but this was readily accounted for when one became acquainted with their refined mother and their independent, high-spirited father. A strong family likeness existed between the boys; but Brer was dark, with dusky eyes and hair, while little Gene was fair, with light hair and blue or "white" eyes, as Brer teasingly called them. Gene was such a "thin-skinned" little fellow that Brer could not resist the temptation to poke fun at him occasionally, just to "toughen" him, he said.

It is true Gene was exceedingly quick to fly into a passion; but his wrath died out as quickly as it came, for Brer knew very well how to manage him. No one could remain angry with Brer long; he was such a clever, good-natured boy. He was Gene's hero and model; the little fellow had been following in his big brer's footsteps, and trying to be just like him, ever since he was a baby and Brer a toddling mischief of two years.

"What do you reckon the bees are saying, Nap?" asked Gene.

"Hum-mum-mum," Nap saucily replied, between his mouthfuls of potatoes.

"Oh, come, now, you Nap, tell us what they say," demanded Brer, making a vigorous pretext of pitching his potato at Nap.

The little darky instinctively ducked his woolly head under his arm, but lifted it instantly with a grin, for he knew very well that Brer had no intention of losing that potato.

"I 'low de bees am keepin' a secret," he replied obediently; and he added, with a sly glance toward the girls, who were playing dolls on the end of the gallery, "Lak Neal and Joy keeps secrets, — mum-mum-mum."

The boys set up a shout at this keen hit at the girls. Joy joined in with a shrill little laugh, for she always enjoyed the boys' jokes, even when at her own expense; but

Neal, who was always trying to get even with the boys, pressed back the smile that twitched her lips and bent low over her doll to hide the twinkle in her eyes.

"If bees keep secrets like girls do, we're bound to find this one out," laughed Brer. "I know something that I sha'n't tell, mum-mum-mum." He pursed up his lips and pressed them hard with his finger, as he had seen the girls do when they wanted to keep a secret in.

Neal looked up defiantly.

"I reckon girls can keep secrets as well as boys," she cried; "this is the way you-all do." She dropped her doll and strutted pompously up and down the gallery. "You swell out just like you would burst if you did n't tell, and your eyes get so big and bright, *so*, that the secret is bound to shine out."

Joy's gleeful laugh rang out again, and the boys laughed too.

"We never looked such idiots as that in our lives," declared Brer.   "If we did, it was only to fool you girls.   When we have a sure-enough secret, no one would ever think it."

"I reckon de bees 'low, ef dey keeps right mum, we-uns neber fin' out whar dey tote de honey," remarked Nap, recalling their attention to the bees.

"They're mighty sharp, but they can't fool us," cried Brer; "I wish the old sun would hurry along."

The boys were waiting, with what patience they could command, for the slow-moving sun to sink so low in his course that his fiery darts should not blind their eyes as they traced the course of the wily bees to their secret storehouse.

It was early in February, when Northern boys are muffled up to their ears in defence against Jack Frost; but the feet of Brer and Gene were as bare as the two black ones that waved in the air. For one of the most delightful things about the water-oaks is that where they grow all the seasons are so warm that the canopy of leaves above is always green, and one can run about barefooted below, all the year round.

To be sure, there are two or three mornings in January when the air is uncomfortably keen, and a thin white coating of frost lies on all the roofs of the Owlets' Roost, the old well-house, the new well-house, the potato-house, the storehouse, the smokehouse, and on the new big barn away to the right of the yard, and on the sheds of the old barn away off to the left, and on the molasses-house halfway between the two barns. But the slight frost usually disappears before sun-up, and one must look sharp to see it. Once or twice in their short lives, the boys had found wonderful ice-crystals shooting across the surface of the water in the bucket on the back gallery; and once, only once, they had seen a snowfall. The sight was so strange that they were almost frightened, and nearly as wild as the chickens that ran distractedly hither and thither pecking at the bountiful fall of flakes that vanished so strangely from the ground.

Just now a thick bed of brown leaves lay around the roots of the water-oaks; for new buds were pushing off the leaves that had shaded the house for a year, and were bursting into the tasselled blossoms around which the bees were swarming.

The sun loitered exasperatingly that afternoon, it seemed to the boys.

"I believe the old thing is standing there on purpose to bother us," exclaimed Gene, the last shred of his patience snapping when the supply of potatoes gave out.

"It's bound to go down sometime," said Brer, encouragingly. "Can you see what time the clock says, Mamma?"

The sun was considered by the family a

more reliable time-keeper than the clock; only when the former failed to keep up with their plans, did the boys deign to consult the capricious timepiece in the room, — a place that they did not frequent except on chilly winter evenings when the north wind drove them from the gallery to the glowing fireplace within.

Only a tiny blaze was fluttering there now, but Mrs. Lee sat in the cosey chimney-corner knitting the white square of a counterpane. At Brer's question she glanced up.

" The clock says half-past four," she replied in her low, sweet voice; " but I reckon it has gained since your father went to town."

" Half-past four! Come on! We won't get round by night if we don't look sharp. I reckon the sun won't out our eyes now. Come on! Come on, you Nap."

It was Brer, by right of his twelve years

and his superior attainments, who planned and directed all the work and fun of the three boys; for Gene was only ten, and Nap was smaller than Gene, and he never had any birthdays.

Usually when they started off for the woods they fell into Indian file, — Brer ahead, Gene following, and Nap contentedly bringing up the rear; but this time, in their search for the bee tree, Brer placed Nap first, for the boys half suspected that he was already in the secret, and as able to take a bee-line to the honey storehouse as the bees themselves.

If he did not already know the secret, he knew how to find it out. The bees were leaving the water-oaks in all directions, but Nap was not to be deceived. He knew that they all were of one swarm, and that they were only making a pretence of separating until they should be away from the house and should think that they had escaped notice, then they would dart straight to one tree.

The boys had left the yard, and trudged for some time in silence down the thicket road, when Nap came to a halt under the dogwood trees.

"Is you gwine bide yer, Brer, an' watch out?"

"I reckon," Brer answered, as if that had been his plan all along.

"Am Gene gwine watch out back ob de cane-patch?"

"I reckon," cried Gene, darting off.

"Does you-all reckon Nap bes' go yonda roun' de pon'?" asked Nap, anxiously.

"Yes; git!" assented Brer, dropping on the pine-straw and tossing a burr at Nap.

The nimble little darky caught the burr, sent it flying back with sure aim, and putting a pine-tree between himself and Brer, sped away to the pond. When he had scurried around the pine-studded brim of the basin, he threw his little body upon a fallen pine log, and pulling the straw crown that served for a hat over his face, he applied a keen eye to one of the many slits in it, to watch for the home-flying bee.

He did not peep long through the chink before he discovered the way to the sly bees' house. There they went, across the disk of blue sky that covered the pond, one little speck and another and more, coming from various directions, but all aiming toward one point.

Nap whistled the mellow notes of the meadow-lark; Brer and Gene instantly responded, and in a few moments came bounding over the pine-straw, demanding excitedly the way to the tree.

"I reckon it am dat-a-way; I reckon you-all see de bees in a minute." He showed them where to watch; and peering up through a telescope made with his hands, Brer soon made out the moving specks.

"Come on!" he cried; and again, with Nap ahead, they sped through the pines.

It did not take them long to find the tree. It was the dead white pine near the rippling branch on the other side of the gully. The bees were buzzing noisily about the tree-top, and the boys could see a black swarm around a hole just above the lowest branch of the tree.

With his jack-knife Brer cut a large B — his mark, and of course a mark for all three boys — in the bark of the tree, to secure it against the claim of any one else who might follow the bees; then they turned homeward in high glee over their success.

Between the bee tree and home, however, lay the gully. There they must loiter awhile, for the gully is the most fascinating playground in the piney woods, and the boys never could pass it without stopping for a frolic.

The gully is a deep crevice in the hillside, probably formed by the washing of a spring in some remote time. Its rim is firm, and bristling with the projecting roots of pines that grow on its edge ; its perpendicular sides are hidden by a tangle of vines and shrubs. Some gum-trees, rooted in the bottom of the gully, brush the sides with their branches in vain effort to reach the top and peep over; but only those trees that have been fortunate enough to secure a footing high on the sides are able to reach far enough to peep out into the piney woods, but they good-naturedly whisper back to their lowly companions all that they see.

The great charm of the gully is a high ridge of clean sand, beautifully shaded from deep reds to delicate flesh-tints. It begins at an abrupt stump-shaped elevation in the middle of the gully, higher even than the sides, and descends in a long line to the mouth, sloping away on both sides in most enticing slides. Across from the edge of the gully to the sand-stump, lies a large pine-tree, hurled there by some accommodating wind.

Across this natural bridge ran Brer and Gene and Nap, balancing themselves with their hands and clinging with their toes, then over they went, tumbling and sliding down the slope of loose, warm sand, to struggle up again for another plunge. There was no jollier sport in the piney woods.

When they were warm and breathless with climbing and tumbling, they took turns being buried in the sand. Finally Brer and Gene covered Nap to his little black chin, so that there was nothing left of him but his woolly head and funny, wrinkled face. His eyes rolled comically up at them, and his white teeth flashed in a continual grin.

" Good-by, Nap."

" Good-by, Brer; good-by, Gene. Take keer yo'self."

Nap remained perfectly still until Brer

and Gene had swung themselves up the gum-trees and disappeared over the edge of the gully. Then the sand about him began to heave and slide like a small earthquake. Presently a black foot cropped up, then its fellow, and both began to kick vigorously. The little quick hands came out and fell to work like lightning in the sand, until the whole boy was unearthed, and sprang with a chuckle to his feet. He gave himself a shake, jammed his tattered straw crown over his wool, and, like a flash, was up the gum-trees.

The boys were galloping on piney-woods ponies in the sapling thicket at the head of the gully. In a trice, Nap was as splendidly mounted as they, on the springing stem of a bent sapling, clinging to the pine-top with one hand, beating unmercifully with the other, prancing wildly up and down at the top of his horse's speed, with such startling screams, "Hi! hi! hi!" that Gene lost his seat and suddenly dipped to the under-side of his slender steed, tearing a long rent in his jean breeches, and scraping his leg most exasperatingly on the rough bark hide.

"You Nap," he shouted angrily, dropping to the ground to nurse the smart, "I'll learn you how to scare a fellow so! I'll have the ha'nt from the graveyard after you some dark night!"

"Law, I did n't go fur to mek yo' hu't yo'self, Gene; I 'low yo' hab a betta holt on yo' ho'se."

Nap had not much fear that Gene would set the "ha'nt" on him, for he knew that the boys were as afraid of the ghost as he was; but he was sorry to have hurt Gene, and sprang from his pony to the ground.

"Pooh! don't be a baby, Gene. Pity if you can't get a scratch without whining," scornfully cried Brer, who was bounding rapturously on a springing pony in supreme indifference to Gene's smart.

"You would n't like it, I reckon," retorted Gene, his face still screwed up with the pain, but rising under his big brer's taunt. "I just wish Nap would get hurt once so he'd know how it feels. But I don't believe you could scratch him with a hoe; I reckon he came out of the alligator-hole, his hide 's so thick."

"Oh, hush your growling and come on!" commanded Brer. Gene made a sudden dart at Nap's sapling.

"I'm going to have this one," he snapped ill-naturedly. "Nap, he always gets the best."

"All right, Gene, I's gwine fin' 'noder," agreed Nap, cheerfully.

"You're so spry, you'd better take the big sapling yonder," Gene cried sarcastically, pointing to a tall sapling that hung, by its loosened roots, far out over the gully.

"I reckon so," replied Nap, taking him at his word, and starting toward the tree.

"Come back, you Nap! Mamma said we should n't swing over the gully," ordered Brer.

Nap paused obediently.

"She never said *Nap* should n't," insisted Gene, perversely.

"That 's so," Brer agreed. He looked longingly at the tree. He sorely longed for the privilege of swinging in that tree; and the next-best thing to going out himself was to see Nap there.

"Sure it will hold ?" he asked.

Nap ran on to the tree, and critically examined its roots.

"I reckon," he called back, waiting eagerly for Brer's permission to go out.

"If you 're sure — I don't care what you do."

"Go it if you dast," challenged Gene.

Nap made a spring, and with knees, feet, and hands climbed up the slender stem and crawled out upon its tapering length until he was perched in the feathery pine-top, far out over the deep gully.

He threw up his arms in the sunshine and gave a shout of delight. He swayed as lightly as a bird on a slender twig; and inspired by the motion, he presently began to chirp and gurgle, and finally he burst forth in a medley of all bird-songs, and warbled away as clearly and blithely as a " sure-enough " mocking-bird.

The boys had often heard his mimicry before; but never had it seemed so charming as now, from the slender, swaying perch.

" That beats old Whir, sure," cried Brer, bouncing from his pony and running to the edge of the gully.

Whir was the boys' own particular mocking-bird, who, in summer, nested with his mate in the scuppernong arbor, pecking grapes by daylight and singing long and loud by moonlight. In winter he and his mate helped themselves to the red holly and dogwood berries hung for them by the boys on the gallery of the Owlets' Roost, and they selfishly fought off all other birds that ventured to approach the water-oaks.

When Nap ended his song, Gene clapped his hands enthusiastically. He had quite recovered from his fit of temper, and he was very proud of their Nap's accomplishments.

But Brer had seen something that made him very sober. He called, —

"Come along *back*, you Nap, and mind you move easy."

Nap started promptly to obey; but at his first movement the tree bent slowly and dangerously low. The boys shouted, and rushed to the roots, that were slowly but surely upheaving, and bore down with all their might upon the upturned earth.

"Go easy, I say," Brer shouted steadily, but his face was as frightened as Gene's.

Nap moved as cautiously as possible; but his light weight was the last straw that overcame the resistance of the roots; and in spite of the boys' efforts to keep it up, the tree went crashing into the gully, dragging an avalanche of earth down with it.

Brer darted back with Gene just in time to save them both from plunging head-first after. He sat down emphatically with the force of backward movement, and Gene sat down beside him. They were on their feet instantly, however.

" Nap 's bound to light on his feet," gasped Gene.

Brer turned without a word, and bounding over the log to the sand-ridge, slid down into the midst of the fallen branches, Gene following closely.

" You Nap !" called Brer, in a voice that was trembling, spite of his efforts to control it.

" Yer I is," answered the soft voice, faint and muffled.

They spied him sitting, a little heap, in a nest of pine-needles. His face was hidden in his arm, and red stains covered his calico waist.

" Where are you hurt ? " asked Brer, scattering the debris and kneeling by his side.

" Dunno," responded the feeble voice.

" Get some water quick ! " ordered Brer.

Gene flew down the gully to the spring that flowed at its mouth, and having folded a magnolia leaf in the shape of a cup, filled it with the sparkling water. That was so little ! He jerked off his waist and dipped it into the spring. With this dripping from one hand and the magnolia cup in the other, he hurried back to the boys.

" It 's his nose ! It 's all swelled up like a mushroom," explained Brer, in great distress. " Here, take a sip, Nap, and let me wipe you off."

Nap lowered his arm from his face and drank eagerly. He showed his white teeth in a momentary smile, that gave such a distressing twist to his swollen, bloody features, and his eyes, almost closed with the swelling, were filled with an expression of such appealing dumb suffering, that Gene burst into tears.

"Doan go fo' to cry, Gene," remonstrated Nap, trying not to wince under Brer's awkward touches.

"Hush!" cried Brer, imperatively; and Gene hushed as best he could.

Brer wiped Nap's face with Gene's wet jacket and took off his own to stanch the blood.

"Now, come on," he said, gently helping Nap to stand. "We 'll tote you home."

"I reckon I 's gwine walk," objected Nap, starting bravely forward. He was so dizzy and blind, however, that he began to totter at once; so Brer and Gene hastily fashioned a seat with their crossed hands, and forced him to sit down upon it.

To mount the sliding sand and cross the log with their burden was out of the question. They turned to the mouth of the gully, made their way around the head of the spring, and climbed the long slope of the hill that ran to the water-oaks. Nap was a little body, but he became a mighty weight before they were halfway home.

Nevertheless they staggered onward, refusing to set him down, or to rest until they mounted the steps of the house gallery and resigned him to their mother's care.

Mrs. Lee tenderly dressed the wounds, and laid Nap away on his pallet in the corner of the Owlets' Roost.

"I have told you not to swing over the gully," she said to the boys.

"You never told N—" Gene began, but he had the shame not to finish this defence.

Gene had been crying bitterly over poor Nap's mishap, with the feeling that the accident was all his own fault, since he had suggested the big sapling.

Brer could have wept too, if he had n't "got past crying;" for he knew that he was greatly to blame, since he might and should have prevented the catastrophe.

Nap himself had not shed a tear. He had endured like a stoic the pain when his wounds were dressed. He had even tried to cheer the boys and comfort Neal and Joy, who looked upon his bruised face with tear-filled eyes.

"I reckon how it'll be all right in the mo'nin'," he faltered, with that painful grimace that he intended for a smile.

But it was not all right in the morning; it never was quite right again. Even after a long time, when his features emerged from the puffed flesh and his eyes opened to their natural size, Nap did not recover his former looks; for in his fall, he had not lighted upon his feet, as Gene had trusted, but he had gone down head-first, striking his nose so violently as to break it.

His nose, to begin with, had been flat and wide, and altogether a sufficiently insignificant feature. By the fall the upper part was mashed flatter than ever; but the end was quaintly pinched and turned up, as if it had been pinched with the fire-tongs. The upward nip gave the drollest expression of pertness to his otherwise docile and cheery face.

Except for the pain, of which he never complained, and which soon passed away, the consequences of the fall were of no importance to Nap. As he was supremely unconcerned about his looks, the turn of his nose did not affect his temper; and he remained the same happy, rollicking little darky as ever, only instead of Nap, the boys called him Nip.

As Nap was not his baptismal name, merely a make-shift for want of a better, the change was of little consequence. In fact, it was quite uncertain that Nip ever had been baptized or properly named. He had come to the Water-Oaks, in the first place, in a very mysterious way. He might have dropped down like a burr or come up like a gopher, for all the children knew to the contrary.

They had found him one morning sitting on a log just without the picket paling, with his chin sunk in his hand and his little old solemn face turned patiently toward the gate.

The dogs were sniffing curiously at him through the pickets, and wagging their tails as if in welcome. This in itself was strange, for usually the dogs were frantic at sight of a darky; and even before sight they would set up an angry barking if they scented one approaching through the woods. But Nap, when he was admitted to the yard, they greeted with the fondest caresses and kisses, and he was soon tumbling among them like a brother.

His little black body was scarcely covered with a red cotton slip that hung in tatters from his shoulders. When questioned, he had but one word to say for himself, and that no one was able to make out; but as it sounded more like " Napoleon " than anything else, they gave him the name of the great emperor, making it " Nap," for short.

He was a curious little creature, — sometimes like a little animal, and at other times so much wiser than themselves that the children did not know what to make of him. He was so keen of sight and hearing and smell that Brer and Gene often had the queer feeling that they were missing half that was going on because their senses were so much duller than Nap's.

In the early springtime Nap would lie

for hours with his ear on the pine-straw, listening, he said, to the johnnies and violets that were creeping up; and he would tell Joy the very day when the sweet little flowers would spring up and open their eyes.

His eyes were as keen as the buzzards' that soar up, up, up, to a mere speck, and peer down between the pines for their prey. Since Nap had no wings, and his world was so small, he had no chance to try his eyesight at such long range as the buzzards, so he used his bright eyes in spying out the hidden secrets of the plants and insects. He discovered a thousand wonders that the boys and Neal and Joy never would have noticed but for him. On the great round trunks of the water-oaks he showed them a perfect garden of growing beauties, which, as they could see when the rains had brightened the moss and lichens, extended far up out on the branches even over the roof-sides of the house. There were myriads of tiny insects swarming in this perpendicular garden; and by putting their ears against the tree, the children could hear the constant rustling of the busy life that went on in the wrinkles of the bark.

The trunks of the water-oaks were so large that it was impossible to climb them without a ladder; but Nap would spring from the cedar-trees at the back of the house to the roof. He would scramble along the ridge-pole, and swinging himself into the oak branches, run along them like a squirrel; and in a twinkling he would be up in the tree-top where the great bunch of mistletoe grew. Away up at that dizzy height, he would wrap his little legs around a branch and swing head downward, or he would drop almost as lightly as a flying squirrel to the lower branches, where he would stand on his head and turn summersaults along their length.

Once the boys had undertaken to "learn" Nap, but the little darky had such a ridiculous way of looking at pictures and of saying his letters upside-down, spite of their efforts to teach him better, that the boys would go into spasms of laughter that sadly interfered with the lessons. This was a pity, for Nap was a·very bright scholar, and very eager to learn; and even with his book wrong-side-up, he made considerable progress.

Nap was puzzled to understand what difference the position of the book made. "A," he pronounced, holding the book properly, as Brer told him. Then he turned the other side up, as he liked it best.

"Am dat *A*, Brer?" he asked with his finger on the same letter.

"Of course it's *A*."

Nap turned the book on one side.

"Am dat *A*?"

"Yes."

He turned to the other side.

“ Am dat *A ?* ”

Brer grinned and nodded.

“ Am dat allus *A*, Brer ? ”

The boys set up a shout at this logical conclusion. It was useless to argue with Nip any longer; and as it was too absurd to teach from a book held upside-down, the lessons came to an end.

Nip knew plenty of things out of books. “ I reckon de moons am de ha’nts ob de suns dat gits bur’d ebry ebnin’ in de pine-trees yonda,” he remarked one night when the moon was peering down at them through the dancing leaves of the water-oaks.

“ What are the stars, Nip ? ” asked Gene.

“ I ’low de stars am de ha’nts ob de sun-beams.” So he had an explanation for all the wonderful things with which their small world was full.

He could tell what the pine-tops were whispering when they waved away up in the blue ; he knew what the leaves of the water-oaks said, and what the squirrels chattered about when they scurried along the branches of the oaks and over the roof of the house. With his wonderful voice he talked with all the birds in their own language. He took his turn with the roosters when they crowed; he imitated Susanna's cackle so exactly that Neal and Joy would fly excitedly to find the egg in the old hen's nest; with a gobble, he could set all the gobblers a-gobbling, and the whole flock of turkeys to strutting and wheeling about the yard in a most comical fashion. He could screech so well that the three geese would come screaming in a great flurry from the pond, with wings a-flapping and heads stretched out to see what fourth goose had come to the Water-Oaks. They were great geese indeed.

Of books, Brer and Gene themselves knew very little. Several times young lady teachers had come into their little world to instruct the boys; and every day for hours they would be shut up in the Owlets' Roost with their books. They submitted very meekly to this imprisonment, and pegged away right faithfully at their lessons, managing to stow away a great many facts to wonder over by themselves and to hurl at Nip's incredulous head.

Of course no one ever thought of sending Nip to school, and Neal and Joy were too young to study; so the two boys had the Owlets' Roost and the teacher all to themselves. Such a school was very monotonous; but, as it happened, their terms of study were very brief, for the poor young ladies soon became homesick shut up in the piney woods, and begged to be returned to the outside world.

The outside world was a great wonder to the children; sometimes they heard a strange rumbling in the east that, their father said, was made by the steamcars at Dewberry bayou; and sometimes they heard the deep whistle of the steamboats in the far-away city. Brer and Gene could tell Nip something about the steamers, for every summer their father harnessed big Pacer into the long wagon and drove, with their mother, the girls, and themselves, twenty long miles through the piney woods to Grandma's Bay. There they splashed in the water, rolled in the sand, and hunted crabs to their hearts' content. And from Grandma's high gallery, that projected quite over the water, they could see the white sails of the ships and the black smoke of the steamers as they passed toward the city, or out again to the gulf.

It was when they were on Grandma's Bay that the boys came nearest to believing that the earth is round; for there was the low, curving horizon, the sky bending like a dome over the water, and the ships creeping up from the other side.

When they returned home, Brer would take a pomegranate and try to make Nip understand how the earth resembles it, and that he was like a fly creeping over it.

Nip did not contradict, — he never was so presuming; but he expressed his doubts of such a ridiculous story by turning a circle of twinkling summersaults.

"Dis yer yearth ob ourn sutenly do *'pear* flat," he would say when he was right-side-up again, and looking critically around.

"An' dis yer sky am mighty nigh flat, suah," he insisted.

"Ef de yearth am roun' down yonda at Grammer's Bay, I reckon you-alls boun' to slide off some day."

The boys ridiculed Nip's ignorance, and insisted upon forcing the truth upon him. He let them argue as long as they pleased, while he only gazed significantly around the level clearing and at the stretch of blue above. The boys looked too, and forgot about Grandma's Bay; and when they had been shut up in their piney wood a few days, they let Nip alone, being too engrossed in enjoying life in their own particular little world around the water-oaks, to concern themselves long about such an impersonal matter as the rotundity of the earth. All their interests centred about the five water-oaks that shelter their home. These great trees stand in the middle of a broad clearing in the piney woods of one of our most southern States; their broad branches stretch protectingly over the house that nestles at their very roots, as gray and lichen-covered as the great trunks themselves. One might think that trees and house had grown up together, so nearly alike are they in color. Certainly there are enough roots for house as well as for trees, for they radiate in long lines through the yard, pushing up through the hard clay in most provoking, stubbing blocks for bare toes.

The house, with the various outbuildings

clustering around it, — the old well-house, the new well-house, the storehouse, the potato-house, the smoke-house, some under the shelter of the water-oaks, others farther out under the pecan and walnut trees, — is protected by a high picket paling, that is pieced out at one corner where the Owlets' Roost stands, half in the yard, half in the old peach orchard.

The fine new barn, much larger than the house, and the low lounging sheds of the old barn and the molasses-house, are entirely outside the paling, removed to a seemly distance.

Pushed far back on all sides of the water-oaks, is a high wall of long-stemmed feathery pines, which entirely surrounds the broad clearing, and encloses the people under the water-oaks in a little world all their own. The clearing outside the picket paling around the house is cut up by criss-cross rail-fences in sections known as the " patches : "

on the side of the new barn are the potato-patch, corn-patch, turnip-patch, greens-patch, oats-patch, watermelon-patch, peach orchard, and garden; on the old barn side is the old peach orchard, including the scuppernong arbor, and the sugarcane-patch. Surrounding all these patches runs one long line of rail-fence along the border of the pines.

A beautiful soft sky canopies this little world, stretching across the clearing from pine-tops to pine-tops; through the blue move glorious suns of various sizes and degrees of splendor. Some days the sun that rises is nearly as large as the top of the old well; while on other days a sun not much larger than the glimmering disk of water at the bottom comes up from the pines. The beams from some suns are so hot that they threaten to shrivel up any one who ventures from the shade of the water-oaks; while other suns beam down with a mild warmth and light that are very grateful. Moons, at night, follow the sun; stars start out in strange array over the patches, or blink knowingly down through the leaves of the water-oaks. Fleecy white clouds sail through the deep azure of the sky; grand thunder-heads loom up in the south; and dark angry clouds come sweeping over the pine-tops from the north, flashing with lightning and crashing with thunder.

With their own little world so fascinating and full of strange happenings, what time had the children to fritter away in speculations about the shape of the outside world?

CHAPTER II.

THE DEER HUNT.

BRER and Gene were on a wild chase after Flo; and Flo with frantic yelps was spinning far ahead over the pine-straw on the track of a round-eyed, bobtailed rabbit.

Suddenly Gene pulled himself up, whirled around in his tracks, and dropped on his knees beside a cluster of salamander hills. He bent for an instant over the soft yellow sand-heaps, and then gave a shrill shout, "Brer! Oh, Brer! Hold on! Just look a-here, will you?"

Brer slowed up with evident reluctance, and with eyes and ears still intent upon Flo.

"What's the matter? Come on! we'll lose it!" and he started on again.

"Oh, *you!*" screamed Gene, dancing up and down in his eagerness. "Let it go, — that *rabbit!* Just you look a-here once! Brer-rer-rer!"

Thus beset, Brer allowed Flo's plumy tail to vanish in the tyty grove at the head of Sweet-Water Branch, and came grumblingly back.

"I reckon you think you're going to show me a pesky salamander this time, sure. Where is he? Come, give us a look at him. It's time for him to show something else than those everlasting sand-burrows. Where is he now?"

Plainly Brer was greatly put out by this interruption of his sport, and indisposed to be satisfied with anything less than a sight of the mysterious salamander which during the nights and the rains threw up myriads of little yellow hills through the pine-straw, but which never had allowed to their watchful eyes the briefest glimpse of its shy head above ground.

Of course Nip had seen it, and so the boys knew what it was like, and what it was not like, — neither like a frog nor a lizard, and something like both.

Had Gene actually succeeded in capturing a salamander, the rabbit might go; but Brer knew very well that Gene could have had no such luck, and he was very angry indeed at losing the rabbit.

Gene gave no heed to his brer's scowls.

"Look a-there!" he cried, pointing triumphantly at the salamander hills.

The indifferent gaze that Brer bent upon the soft sand-mounds suddenly became eager. His face flushed and his brown eyes sparkled with excitement as he stooped down and examined the dainty tracks that marked the moist sand-hill.

"A deer, sure," he murmured in a suppressed voice.

"Of course it's a deer!" screamed Gene.

"Hush, goose; you'll run it off," commanded Brer. "Don't you see that the tracks are right fresh?"

With the instinct of a true hunter he cocked his gun and peered cautiously around. There was no live creature to be seen except Flo, who came loiteringly toward them, with lolling tongue and tail hung low, and with a very clear expression of wonder and reproach in her eyes at their base failure to follow up the bunny which she had so nearly run down for them. The boys' only explanation of their strange conduct was to thrust her pointed nose into the deer-tracks. The little dog gave instant recognition of the fresh scent by a series of sharp barks; and after nosing about a while, quivering with excitement, she started straight off toward the enclosure called the " pasture," giving a quick yelp every now and then as she followed the trail. The boys trotted close at her heels, their guns cocked, and their keen glances flashing ahead for a first glimpse of the game. It was glorious to feel that at last they were on a "sure-enough" hunt, with a good prospect of bringing down a deer, — a deer! They panted and trembled with excitement, but there! They had gone but a few rods when the horn sounded from the house. At the well-known summons all three stopped short, Flo with a howl of remonstrance, and the boys with groans of despair. The brown eyes and the blue exchanged one rebellious flash; then the boys broke away from the chase and ran rapidly toward the house. It was exceedingly hard for them to leave that deer, and the tears of disappointment welled in Brer's eyes; but he manfully winked them back, and hushed Gene, who was fairly fuming with rage, and whose blue eyes actually seemed to snap out sparks of angry fire.

"I bet one of the girls winded that horn just to fool us!" he cried. "If they did — "

"No, they never. It's Mamma. It's time. Look yonder; it's almost sundown. We won't get the work done by dark."

"But a deer! It's right mean to have to leave it," sputtered Gene. Then he turned and shouted savagely, at the top of his voice, "You, Flo! here, come here! you Flo! *Flo!*"

But Flo flew on with a yelp. She knew as well as the boys knew that the horn was an imperative summons to the house. Her instinct, however, was stronger than her sense of obedience; after a moment's hesitation at the sound of the horn, she had whined wistfully along the trail, and finally had broken bonds, and now was in full cry after the deer. She paid no attention to the boys' shouting and whistling.

"Go stop her; she 'll run the deer off," cried Brer, himself keeping on toward the house.

"I 'll stop her, the hard-headed beast!

She needs a lesson, and she 'll get it," shouted Gene, bounding after Flo, yelling wrathfully at the wilful little dog.

Flo heard him following, and half paused; but the trail was hot, and the keen scent drew her onward, spite of herself. She was confused, however, by his cries, and slackened her pace so that Gene soon managed to shorten the distance between them. Still she refused to abandon the trail and return as he ordered; and at last, out of breath from running, and furious at her disobedience, the boy lifted his gun and fired at her. Poor Flo made one bound, then howling with pain, whirled rapidly round and round. When Gene, white and shocked at his deed, ran coaxingly up to her, she crouched low, and with her tail between her legs, and with piteous whining, shrank away from him and limped skulkingly toward home.

Horrified and ashamed of his passionate

act, Gene hurried after the yelping little creature. Before he reached home, Brer came rushing out to meet him.

"What's the row?" he demanded breathlessly. "What did you shoot at? Did you see the deer, sure enough?"

Gene could only shake his head.

"What was it, then? What ails Flo? She's just slunk under the house and is whining like a baby."

"I shot her," gasped poor Gene, pulling his hat over his face and bursting into convulsive sobs.

"Shot Flo!" exclaimed Brer, gazing upon the grief-shaken little figure of his brother with amazement. "You — shot — Flo! Gee! What did you do that for, I'd like to know?"

"She wouldn't stop, and I was mad," wailed Gene, stumbling over a pine-knot as he made his way blindly along.

Brer took possession of the gun, and

grasped Gene's limp hand. He was dumfounded and almost as disturbed as Gene at the occurrence. He led him along without a word for a while; then he exclaimed abruptly, "Suppose it had been buck-shot!" at which suggestion Gene's grief broke forth afresh.

"I never thought I'd hit her," he sobbed.

"No, I reckon not, I reckon you didn't think anything; but you did hit her, you see. Suppose it had been Nip or me, I reckon it wouldn't have made a bit of difference. You'd done us just the same as you did Flo. I declare, you 're right dangerous with a gun!"

"Oh, I don't want a gun; I'll never touch one again!" cried Gene, actually frightened by the thought of the awful things he might do in one of his blind passions.

He threw himself upon the ground in a paroxysm of fear and remorse.

"I don't want to shoot anybody," he moaned; "I did n't go for to shoot Flo."

Brer was alarmed at the storm of passion that shook his little brother; and kneeling down, he put his arms around the trembling form and began to soothe him. "Oh, come, now; don't take on so, Gene. Of course you did n't mean to do it; and I reckon Nip and I are safe enough. I 'll trust you not to shoot us, nor anybody nor anything. I reckon you 've learned a lesson, and you 're safe not to do that way again. Come on, now, Mamma will think you are hurt, and will be coming out to see. Come, I reckon Flo is more frightened than hurt. Besides, there is all the work, and it is sundown now."

Thus coaxed and urged, Gene allowed himself to be lifted to his feet and trotted along beside his brer, with a penitent, tear-stained face and with an occasional sniff to tell of his repressed feelings.

His grief and shame burst forth again at sight of his mother, who was anxiously waiting at the gate. Rushing to her, he clasped her convulsively, and with loud sobbings buried his face in her bosom.

She held him close, alarmed at the outburst, and looked to Brer for explanation.

"He got provoked and peppered Flo with small-shot," Brer said briefly.

"My son did that? My son! My poor little son let the angry spirit get the better of him, so that he hurt an innocent dumb beast! Mother is ashamed and sorry."

She did not loosen her warm clasp, but led him away to her room, bidding Brer go on with his work, promising that his little brother should join him in a few minutes.

"Can't Nip water the horses?" asked Brer.

"Well, yes, I reckon he might, if he'll be careful not to get a tumble. Tell him not to mount."

Mrs. Lee gave this permission with some hesitation; for Nip was still an invalid, with his nose under a plaster, and he had been kept very quiet lest some new injury should befall him.

Brer could hear Nip and the girls laughing on the front gallery, and he stole slyly to the corner of the house to see what amused them.

It would be very unjust to Neal and Joy to say that they rejoiced over Nip's broken nose, for no little girls could have been more tender-hearted and sympathetic than they had been while the throbbing pain lasted; but without doubt they enjoyed the novelty of having Nip about the house, and derived the greatest pleasure in nursing him. Certainly two little girls never devoted themselves to a more charming and diverting patient.

It is true that except when one or the other took a notion to dose him with some home-made concoction, such as pine-top tea, sassafras tonic, or dogwood berry wine, they usually forgot his invalid condition; for the little darky had the most entertaining habit of assuming one character after another in bewildering succession.

At one time he would be a stupid owl, solemnly blinking at them from a dark corner and startling them with a sudden "Too-whit, too-whoo," or by flapping awkwardly across to another corner.

At another time he was down on all fours in comic imitation of Neal's pet Nanny, pattering briskly up and down the galleries, marching smartly through the rooms, nibbling at everything within reach, papers, books, the splint bottoms of chairs, the dolls' dresses,— everything, in fact, which the girls could not whisk out of the way. Not until Neal called him off would he pause in his mischievous incursions; and then he would patter around after his little mistress with

a persistency that drove Neal frantically
hither and thither in vain efforts to escape, and which caused Joy to scream with
laughter.

"Baa, baa!" the little black Nan would
bleat, until Neal would seize his wool and
drag him with pretended force into an imaginary orchard; and even then, the importunate bleating would continue until a
bottle full of milk and water had been
brought. Seizing the nipple in his mouth,
he would pull and butt away in the most
vigorous Nanny-fashion until the bottle
was emptied, and Neal and Joy exhausted
with laughing.

There was no creature nor person under
the water-oaks whose character he did not
assume during his enforced stay at the house.
When Brer sought him, he was swaying
serenely back and forth in a rocking-chair
on the front gallery. Poised lightly in his
slender hands was a set of knitting-needles

that were flashing briskly through some bright wool. At his feet sat Neal and Joy, at whom he was peering over a pair of imaginary spectacles with an expression of mild benevolence that could not be mistaken. He was Grandma for the time being.

"Neal, my deah," he was saying with gentle severity, "set right up, chile; it 'stresses me to see yo' ches' so narrer. You-alls gwine be roun' lak a bar'l-hoop, ef you doan watch out. I reckon you wants to be straight an' el'gant lak yo' aunty. Now, den, dat am betta. Joy, lob, doan wiggle yo' li'l' body 'bout so. Yo' 'stract yo' po' grammer so she can't go long wiv dis yer story. Dar, dat am right puty. Now, den, whar did Grammer git to? Oh, yas, I 'members. 'Now when dis yer li'l' bird wat I done tole yo' 'bout —'"

"Come along, Grandma, and help me with the horses," here broke in Brer, in a disrespectful shout.

“Oh, Brer, what ails Flo?” screamed the girls, in a shrill duet. “She’s under the house whining, and won’t come out.”

“Flo! who said there was anything the matter with Flo?” demanded Brer.

“But something is the matter. Nip crawled under, and she would n’t let him touch her, and she ’s fond of Nip, you know. What did hurt her? What did you shoot?”

“I ’m in a hurry; come on, Grammer,” was Brer’s only response.

“He can’t come until you tell about Flo,” declared Neal.

“Yes, he can. Mamma said he was to help me.”

“Well, he can go when he tells what became of the little bird.”

“Oh, don’t mind them, Nip, come on.”

Nip, who had preserved his dignity throughout this squabble, raised a slender hand in quiet rebuke. “Li’l’ chilluns, li’l’ chilluns, gently! Brer done forgot hisself when he done 'terrupt his ole grammer so, an' tell her come 'ten' de ho'ses. I's too ole to 'ten' de ho'ses, Brer; but I 'low I ken sen' dat lazy nigger, Nip, to help yo' ef I ken fin' de no 'count rascal. Jes' go 'long, Brer; I 'low he's comin'."

"Now, Nip, you can't — "

"Hush, Neal. Dat dar li'l' bird jes' go up an' up, pas' de sky. I's comin', Brer!"

"What did the little bird find up there past the sky?" persisted Joy.

"Go 'long, Joy. Dis chile dunno. I's gwine fin' out some day, I reckon, when I done wata de ho'ses."

He slipped away from the unwilling girls and spun away across the yard and out to the new barn.

"Das we let 'em hab a run dis ebnin', Brer?" he asked, as he let out old Bess and her colt to find their own way to the trough.

"No, not to-night. It's almost dark now. Just hurry along as fast as ever you can. I'm just bound to have some fun to-night. I'll tell you. Perhaps Mamma'll let you go with me. Just hustle the horses along. What's that Bess up to? You Bess, whoa there!"

The old horse was nosing the wooden latch of the gate, with the intention of entering the yard and taking a stroll around the house under the water-oaks; but at Brer's authoritative call she tossed her black mane with a show of indifference and hurried demurely back to the trough, her colt frisking around her.

Next to the stall of old Bess was that of Pacer, who was stamping about impatiently. Pacer was a high and mighty horse in more senses than one. He was a great tall, strong creature with a temper as fiery as his red coat. Indeed, he was of such vicious temper that before Nip came, no one but Mr. Lee had ventured to approach him; but Nip, at the very first, to the amazement of the boys, had run fearlessly into the stall, tumbled into the hay directly under the horse's fiery eyes and strong gleaming teeth, and had clambered all over the huge beast; and Pacer had endured all this familiarity without once bucking or lifting a hoof.

" Come 'long, old Pacer," sang Nip, swinging open the door of the stall and reaching up to clutch the long red mane as the horse hurried out.

Pacer tossed his head with a whinny and trotted to the trough, Nip running at his side. "Brer 'low yo'-all carn't hab no frolic dis ebnin', ol' Pacer. Marster done go on de hunt, and we-uns doin' all de wo'k," explained Nip, patting the horse's smooth neck while he drank. But Pacer was tired of confinement and eager for a race. He shook his head, impatient of restraint; and lifting his plumy tail like a challenging signal, he started off smartly for the woods.

"No yer doan, Mars Pacer. Jes' yo' tote yo'self back to de ba'n."

The little darky had kept his hold of the mane; and now, with amazing agility, he managed to swing himself up on the broad back of the horse.

"Now, whoa, sah, whoa — whoop! Go long back to de ba'n, lak I tole yo'." He tugged at the mane and pounded Pacer's hard sides with his bare heels.

The horse hesitated a moment, when the light weight rested on his back, then with a snort of disappointment, wheeled about and galloped straight back to the barn and entered his stall.

" You 's got right good sense, Mars Pacer; I 's mighty obleeged to yo' fo' doin' lak I tole you. I reckon yo'-alls ho'ses ken hab a run to-morrow ebnin'."

In turn, Nip led out the other horses: Jinny, the pet of her master and the easiest saddle-horse in the piney woods; then the race-horse, who had been left with a limping gait and a promise of the record of an illustrious pedigree by a sharp horse-dealer; and finally old yellow Nag, the patient family horse of all work, — the only horse of any account on the place, Mamma, Grandma, and Aunty thought. Each horse, as it left the water-trough, cast a longing look toward the woods, and obeyed reluctantly when Nip's guiding hands turned it back to the barn.

"I knows it am mighty ha'd on yo'; but I reckon nobody carn't help it. Ole Muley-Mule jes' hab to do de trottin' fo' yo'-alls," said Nip, sympathetically, as he bolted old Nag into her stall.

"Heah, yo' good-fo'-not'in' Muley-Mule, what fo' yo' lazin' roun' all day an' night? Gee up, gee up! Hi! hi! hi!" He threw up his hands and dashed screaming at poor Muley-Mule, who was nibbling weakly at the bark of a pine stump.

The old mule looked up in astonishment at this fierce onset, but showed no disposition to move until a bristling pine-burr came whack against her loosely covered ribs. At this insult she lifted her long ears defiantly, and threw up her weak old legs in a manner that was intended to be very threatening indeed, but which was only ridiculously feeble and grotesque.

"Hi! hi! hi!" screamed Nip again, pitching another relentless burr.

Thus pricked into action, Muley-Mule, with an angry flirt of her tasselled tail, and with a desperate leap, started off into the pines with the agility of a colt, as if to show that her spirit was not broken, though her ribs were so prominent and her legs so stiff.

Poor Muley-Mule's strength of limb was not equal to her strength of will, however; her energy departed as suddenly as it came. She completed a short circuit at a slow walk and dragged herself feebly back to the trough ; for there was one thing for which Muley-Mule might be grateful, — if she only had thought of it, — and that was the abundant supply of water with which she might moisten her shrivelled old carcass as often as she chose.

"Dat am a mighty peart showin' up fo' sech an ole empty critter lak yo' is," commended Nip, caressing the mule's rough hide with a stick. "I 's gwine ask Brer lemme gib yo' a year ob co'n, case yo' sech a fine race-ho'se."

At this moment Gene came running out, subdued and kind from his grief over his shameful treatment of Flo ; and feeling anxious to make amends for his cruelty, he declared that poor old Muley-Mule must have some oats. He brought a heaping measure from the bin and emptied it into a concave piece of bark that lay conveniently at hand.

"Yo' is boun' to ask a blessin' on dat ar suppa, suah," exclaimed Nip, delightedly, squatting on the ground to watch the astonished mule enjoy the treat.

Gene hurried into the barn to help Brer, who was shelling corn with all his might.

"Are you going out after supper?" Gene asked rather shamefacedly.

"If Mamma will let us."

"I reckon she won't let *me*; but there's Nip. He might go, if you ask Mamma; 't won't hurt him, and — and he could take my gun." Gene blushed scarlet as he made this offer, and he was obliged to wink his eyes very hard; for it was a sore trial to give up his beloved gun and let the boys go off for that deer without him. Was n't it *his* deer? Had n't he found the tracks?

Brer was too excited to notice Gene's depression. His one thought was to shoot that deer and have a treat of venison for his father and the other hunters when they should return empty-handed, as was often the case, from the camp hunt to which they had gone a week ago. The horns — well, he would keep those himself, since it would be his first deer, but Aunty should have the skin, as he always had promised.

"No," he said in the low tone he always used when excited, "we don't want your gun; Nip'll have to carry the light, you know, and I'll follow on behind, and when I see the critter's eyes, I'll just — bang!" Brer took aim and fired with a corn-cob in a most expressive manner, and gave a whoop of triumph and glee that made the lump in poor Gene's throat swell most uncomfortably; but the little fellow gulped back his grief, for he knew that he had forfeited all right to the deer. Brer's success would be as great a triumph for him as if he should kill the deer himself. He swelled with pride as he imagined Brer exhibiting a pair of enormous buck-horns to the astonished hunters upon their return, empty-handed, of course, from the grand camp hunt, and the delicious venison that would be served to them, and the praises they would sound until Brer's face would be all aglow with shy smiles and blushes, in spite of his efforts to seem unconcerned and to pass it off as no great feat. "Just a scared deer! If it had been a bear, now!" Brer would say.

Gene could fancy just how it would be. He entirely forgot his own disappointment and fell to planning and anticipating with as much eagerness as Brer.

They managed to finish the work in time to fashion a rude sort of lantern, such as they had heard their father tell of using when he and his brothers were boys, and the piney woods abounded in sport, — in the days when deer were so plentiful that a herd of tame deer was kept around the house for the purpose of enticing the shy wild ones within easy range of the concealed hunters.

But those good times when game came oblig-ingly to the very gate of the house were long since past. A deer-track had not been seen within a mile of the water-oaks for years.

When the supper-horn summoned them, the boys bore the lantern to the house and exhibited it with much pride and no little anxiety to their mother. They were by no means sure that she would favor Brer's plan of a night hunt.

Mrs. Lee smiled a little at the dark-lan-tern, which was simply a large tin can, cut open and spread, and fastened around the top of a small pine-torch in such a way as to act as a reflector. She became serious at once, however, when Brer divulged his pro-ject of rousing the curiosity of the deer with the light and enticing it within the rays of the flambeau reflector.

In the first place, she was very incredulous about there being a deer anywhere around, especially in the pasture; but the boys were so confident of the tracks which they had seen that she passed that question by.

"Well, suppose there is a deer, how does Brer propose to manage both gun and light? I don't like to think of him wandering about alone out there in the dark woods, — not that there is anything to hurt him, but he might become confused and wander off."

"I could n't get lost with my eyes shut, Mamma; I 'll go to Cousin Will's any time you say, with a bandage over my eyes. Why, I 'm as sure of my bearings at night as in the daytime. Besides — " and here he hesitated. "I allowed you would n't mind letting Nip go along to carry the light. He *could n't* get hurt; and you know, Mamma, you could n't lose him if you tried."

"I 'low Nip doan know 'nough to lose hisself," here softly observed the little darky, who was lying in the dining-room doorway patiently waiting, while the family ate supper, for his own allowance, which was sure to be choice and ample ; for the children vied with one another in saving delicate tit-bits from their own plates for their cunning little playfellow.

"I reckon dis yer know-nuffin' li'l' nigga doàn hab no mo' sense dan to mek tracks straigh' fo' home, lak de ole pied cat dat jump out ob de bag when yo' fader done tote 'er 'long to drown 'er in deep hole," concluded Nip, voice and eyes expressing intense disgust at the old cat's stupidity in coming home when such pains had been taken to get rid of her.

"Oh, Mamma knows we can't get lost. She 's only fooling. Why, I 've been out to the pasture hundreds of times after dark in cattle-time."

"But you had Papa !" argued Neal, with her dark eyes wide and serious ; for her lively imagination always pictured the dark full of all sorts of dreadful creatures.

"No, he never," contradicted Gene. "*He* does n't need Papa to scare off the bugaboos, like you do. Neither does Joy; *she* is n't a coward. You das n't go out to the orchard gate alone, I bet."

"Yes, I dast too," retorted Neal, defiantly, but shrinking from her chair to her mother's side, as she peered out over her shoulder into the night that had settled down so black that even the trunks of the water-oaks were invisible.

Mamma pressed her fanciful little daughter reassuringly to her; but she asked with a quizzical smile, as she looked into Neal's face, "How would it do for Neal to carry the torch? She has n't a broken nose to be careful of."

"No, but she'd break it, sure, running for her life if once she saw that deer's eyes staring at her out of the dark," cried Brer, derisively. "I 'd rather have nobody than Sister. She 'd drop that torch and out it just the very second when I'd be taking aim. Oh, you're going to let Nip go, I know, Mamma; you're only teasing. Here, you Nip, just you bolt that supper as fast as ever you can."

Nip seized the heaped plate that Brer handed down to him and fell to eating with a right good-will.

"Save room for the venison, you'd best, Nip," said Gene, who was trying hard not to beg that he might go. He couldn't help thinking that his mother might give her permission at the last minute.

"Nip can wear my Mardi-Gras mask; then I reckon he couldn't hurt his nose," whispered Neal, in her mother's ear. She knew very well that her mother never meant to have her go; and yet she was frightened by the very suggestion, and she was eager to do all in her power to secure to Nip the pleasure that she did not crave. After a while she meant to find out why Gene was so strangely left out of the plans. Already her active mind had half guessed the trouble with Flo; for she had a way of putting this and that together when her curiosity demanded information.

Joy's eyes were more snapping and straightforward; but they did not see as keenly into things as Neal's soft, dreamy orbs.

"What *you* going to do, Gene?" she asked, leaning over in her high-chair to pat the cheek of her favorite brother, who sat so silently beside her.

"Stay at home," he tried to answer indifferently; but as four pairs of brown eyes were turned upon him compassionately, his blue eyes suddenly swam in tears.

Joy's eyes filled in instant sympathy; and she looked anxiously at her mother when Neal asked, "*Why* don't Gene go, Mamma?"

"Gene is going to stay with you and me and — with Flo," answered Mrs. Lee.

"*I* know," said Neal. "He done had a tantrum this evening; and that's what ails Flo."

"You *think* you know a *heap*," cried poor Gene.

"I reckon he could n't help it, Mamma," pleaded Joy, with trembling lip.

"He'd better learn to help it, and that right soon. He's getting dangerous," exclaimed Brer.

"I reckon temper goes with white eyes; that's why he's so awfully touchy. Don't you, Mamma?" asked Neal, speculatively.

"As if eyes had anything to do with temper!" chuckled Brer. "Oh, come along, Nip. You won't be able to budge if you down all that hominy."

"I 'low yo' maw done forgit fo' to say yes," loudly whispered Nip behind his hand.

"Mamma dear, you said yes, did n't you?"

"No, my son, but I will say it now. You

and Nip may go, if you will be very prudent, and will promise not to be out longer than an hour and a half, and to come straight home if I wind the horn earlier."

"I *always* come; anyway, we won't be long. You-all just listen for the gun, and then watch out to see some fine venison. How in the world are we going to bring the critter home when we've got him? Never mind, we're bound to manage it."

Having made full preparations, Brer and Nip started forth on the deer hunt. They entered the pasture and cautiously made their way across it toward the ford of Sweet-Water Creek, where, they concluded, the deer would be.

Nip marched on before, steadily bearing above his head the shielded torch, the light of which cast a bright narrow path on the pine-straw before them. His own erect little figure was well shadowed by the cunning contrivance of the can; and Brer, following a few paces behind, was also invisible in its shadow. The dark-lantern worked like a charm, throwing all light before, and leaving everything out of range of its eye in total obscurity.

The yellow light glanced from one scaly pine stem to another and sometimes flickered among the mysteriously whispering pine-tops.

"Watch out sharp, now! Don't you dare to wink! I would n't lose that deer for — Gee! I thought that was it, sure. Go on."

Brer gave his commands in an intense whisper; for the most part, however, he remained quiet, allowing Nip to follow his own will, for he had almost as much faith in the little darky's instinct as he had in Flo's. He was all aglow with excitement; his right hand trembled as it clutched his rifle; every sense was strained and alert. He started at the sound of a crackling twig and at the dropping of an invisible pine-burr; while every shadow that stirred in the bright path of their torch seemed the fleeting form of a deer. Once Nip stubbed his toe and stumbled a little. In an instant Brer's gun was at his shoulder; he lowered it with a long quivering breath. " I declare, I like to have shot you for the deer ! " he gasped.

" I 'low yo'-alls doan wan' waste yo' shot," Nip whispered back over his shoulder. He had been moving steadily ahead without making any response to Brer's exclamation; but not a sound nor a sight had escaped his keen attention. At last, however, he paused with lifted hand, and listened intently.

" Somet'ing, suah," he breathed, concealing himself behind a pine-tree and letting the light fall upon the path that here descended to Sweet-Water Branch.

Brer drew back into the darkness and waited with baited breath. His hand was quite steady now : all danger of an attack of the buck-ague, that is apt to set young hunters a-shivering, was over. He heard the approaching tread of hoofs ; the animal came near, hesitated, advanced a few paces. They could hear its irregular breathing and its curious sniffing, as it tried to make out the nature of the unnatural light before venturing nearer. It was terribly exciting to feel the game so near and yet be unable to catch the faintest glimpse of it ; but Nip held the torch without a quiver of his arm, and Brer kept himself well in check without moving a muscle. How he longed, though, to bang straightway at that breathing, invisible creature in the darkness ! What if that deer should take to its heels, and he should lose his game from under his very hand ! In another instant his self-control would have failed him, and he would have fired blindly into the dark ; but the animal moved, advanced slowly, its two eyes caught the

"I 'low, Brer, how we-alls done kill Neal's heifer."—*Page* 87.

light of the torch, and glowed like two burning coals in the blackness.

Brer ·touched the trigger; the deed was done; the sharp report of the gun, a heavy fall, and a long deep sigh.

Nip gave a yell and sprang forward; Brer followed with a proud sense of triumph that was almost suffocating.

" A sure dead deer, Nip?" he asked, trying to speak coolly.

Nip made no reply; but there in the light of the torch lay the poor thing, quite motionless; but — Brer gasped and stared at Nip in utter bewilderment.

Nip returned his gaze for a moment, and then looked back at the prone form at their feet.

" I 'low, Brer, how we-alls done kill Neal's heifer."

CHAPTER III.

NEAL'S NEW NANNY.

IT was some time before Brer could realize the enormous blunder that he had made. He seized the torch from Nip's hand, dropped to his knees, and gazed at the pretty little heifer as if he could not and would not believe his eyes. He felt the silky ears with his fingers; he took hold of the graceful horns and even shook them a little, as if to test whether they really were the ones that he had seen bud and grow on Lodi's gentle head. He passed his hand over her smooth brown coat, and finally he examined the hoofs; there indeed was the white left hind-foot, Lodi's mark.

When at last the awful truth forced itself upon him, that he had killed Neal's heifer, he staggered to his feet and stared in a dazed way into the dark woods; but after this moment of uncertainty he recovered himself with a start.

"Come on, Nip, let's go to Mamma," he faltered; and turning abruptly, he marched straight back to the Water-Oaks, Nip trotting silently behind him.

Gene was waiting in breathless impatience at the back gate, but Brer pushed by him without a word. Neal and Joy began to scream at him before he was halfway across the yard, but he paid not the least attention to them, nor did he notice the pack of dogs that sprang fawningly around him; he marched straight up the gallery steps and crossed directly to the· door of the room through which was pouring a brilliant flood of light.

"Mamma, I done shot Neal's heifer; she can have Beauty instead." He was going on manfully to explain; but he suddenly be-

came aware that his father and the other
hunters were sitting before the fire, and that
all eyes were turned upon him.   He whirled
about and darted for refuge to the Owlets'
Roost.   There he threw himself upon the
bed in the dark, burying his burning face in
the pillow; and though he *was* "past crying,"
two or three tears would force their way between his closed eyelids, as they had sufficient excuse for doing in such distressing
circumstances.

What could have occurred more mortify-
ing to such a proud-spirited boy as Brer?
After all his vain boastings, to make such a
mistake as to take a heifer for a deer, —
Lodi, at that!   How ashamed he was!   He
could n't bear to think.   He jumped up angrily and turned a dozen savage summersaults to divert his mind.   Then, with fierce
determination, he began to practise walking
around the room on his hands.   Again and
again he came whacking down on the hard

pine floor; but he would not give up before he was able to make the circuit of the room without a fall.

By that time he was so knocked up that he was glad to undress and crawl into bed (the boys and Nip were the owlets that occupied the roost when there was no teacher to hold possession of the little house). To engage his thoughts and keep his attention from the commotion in the yard, he tried to think over some old lessons, and say some poetry that he had learned for his teachers; but he knew them so well that he could repeat them without thinking. The sounds in the yard he could not help listening to, and he could tell from them exactly what was going on out there.

"Quit your listening, you goose!" he commanded himself; but he found that he was not so subject to his own orders as were Gene and Nip.

Finally he heard the smokehouse door

close with a bang, and then the hunters laughing as they noisily mounted the gallery steps and entered the house; and presently Gene and Nip came stealing quietly into the roost.

"I 'll let them think I 'm asleep," thought Brer; but he was too feverish and curious to keep quiet. He pulled himself up in bed, and sat upright in the dim light that was filling the room from the moon which was just rising in full splendor behind the pines.

"They 've done skinned it and dressed it, and Papa said the meat 's bound to be fine," burst forth Gene, as soon as he saw that his brother was awake.

"Neal 'low how she gwine like beef betta dan ven'son," said Nip, consolingly, as he tumbled down on his low pallet.

"Yes, Neal she had to bawl some, of course," went on Gene, loftily, as if he had a right to scorn such babyishness; "but she quit when Mamma said you 'd offered to give her Beauty, and bimeby when Papa asked her, she said she'd rather have the next Nanny he found than Beauty, 'cause nobody could mistake a Nanny for a deer."

"Did you tell them about the tracks?" asked Brer.

"You bet I did! and they just laughed. As if we don't know a deer's track when we see it! I'd just like to show them!" Gene had forgotten all about his own woful experience under the new excitement. "Cousin Will said it was a lucky hit for them. He thinks there's no venison going like tender beef; and he 'lowed the hunters going to camp down here and get fed up. They're just starved; they ate the safe empty, — every last cold potato and all!"

"Did n't they kill a thing?"

"Just one wild-cat. They got on the trail of a bear too,—the biggest fellow, that's just been a-feasting off lambs and honey. Uncle Jim's all tore to pieces a-chasing it through the swamp; but they could n't get a shot. They 're going again pretty soon, though."

Gene made a run and a spring over Brer to his own side of the bed.

"Say, Brer, would n't it be a lark if *we* should kill a bear?" he exclaimed, as he fitted himself comfortably into his own particular hollow.

"I reckon a bar' boun' git in de pasture bimeby," murmured Nip, sleepily, from his corner.

Neither of the boys had a word to say in response to this happy suggestion. Profound silence settled down over the Owlets' Roost; but it did not last long, for presently it was disturbed by the soft regular breathing of Gene, who had slipped wearily into dreamland. Soon.Brer and Nip followed him; and three loud distinct snores resounded through the moon-lit room.

Brer awoke with a start the next morning. He thought that some one had called him. The first thing that he saw was Nip perched on the footboard of the bed, flapping his arms in the very act of echoing the old rooster's "screech of dawn."

"Mo'nin', Brer," he said in polite salutation, when he saw that Brer was doing his best to open his eyes. "'Pears lak yo' doan wan' de ole sun to show hisself so yerly. But yonda he comes, climbin' up de pines lak he gwine bide all day."

"Who called me, Nip?"

"I doan yere nobody callin' yo'; I jes' yere yo' pa argafyin' wiv ole Pacer in de ba'n."

"Is Papa up?" Brer sprang up with a bound that shook Gene out of his morning nap.

His bright eyes were open wide on the instant; and he tumbled briskly out of bed.

"My! it's cold," he cried, shrinking up and shivering.

"It is that!" agreed Brer, hurrying into

his clothing. "My things are right wet with the fog. Just see it pouring in at that window, will you?"

"It's gwine hunt itself togeder an' fly back yonda," observed Nip, pointing to the sky, "ef de ole sun doan bu'n it up."

"I should n't mind floating up on a cloud some day," exclaimed Gene, enthusiastically, looking out at the mist that already was gathering and rising over the patches. "I'd take my gun, and I'd just go a-sailing over the pines; and I'd peek down, and when I saw a herd of deer browsing away, — boom! boom! — there would be two dead deer, sure! I say, though, we're going to have venison for break— Oh no, I forgot;" and Gene relapsed into gloomy silence, for he suddenly remembered.

From the moment when he had opened his eyes, Brer had been oppressed by a strange feeling that something was wrong; but there had not been time for him to decide what was the matter when Gene's words brought back with painful reality the mishaps of the day before.

For one instant the thought occurred to him that he might "take to the woods" until the hunters had left the Water-Oaks; but he was no coward, and he dismissed the idea of running away with scorn.

"Anyway," he thought, "it was n't anything *wrong*; and I bet any one would have done just as I did. It makes a fellow feel cheap, though; and I 'm mighty sorry it was Lodi, but I did n't go for to do it, and I ain't going to skulk."

He ran bravely out to his father, who was feeding the horses in the barn.

"Well, son," was Mr. Lee's greeting, "you got badly fooled yesterday. I reckon you 'd give a picayune if you could take back that shot."

"Yes, sir, I 'd give a heap of picayunes. I 'm right sorry about Lodi."

"So am I. She was bound to make a fine cow. But what's done can't be undone; and she'll make fine beef. I reckon you can manage to make things square with your sister."

"I said I'd give her Beauty; she's a sight prettier than Lodi."

"Well, settle it between yourselves."

Brer went about his work, much cheered by his father's kindness.

His courage received another boost when Neal came skipping out to the old well where he was filling the horse-trough, and assured him in the most sisterly fashion that she did n't mind one bit; she knew he did n't "go for to do it." She was n't going to take Beauty either. Papa had said she might have another Nanny; and *she* thought lambs were a *heap* nicer than cows, and she just *loved* beef. She wished *breakfast was ready.*

It seems rather savage in Neal to be so

ravenous to devour her beloved heifer; but the children under the water-oaks were quite accustomed to seeing their pets go into the pot, from the Nannies that they raised on the bottle to the wee-wees that they took under their own wings, when the hen-mothers refused to care for their broods. Indeed, it was quite understood by Neal and Joy that in due time their dear hen Susanna would be cooped and fattened, and served in a delicious pot-pie; and though they loved Susy with all their hearts, the thought of her tragic fate never saddened them in the least, nor would they relish her drum-sticks any the less for having loved her so dearly.

When the breakfast gong sounded, Brer was quite braced up, so that he could take the chaff of the hunters in the frank, good-natured fashion that they liked; but though he tried not to show his feelings, they did manage to tease him considerably.

"Here you are, Brer! Come around and shake, can't you? You show right good sense when you let deer slip and bring in beef," cried Cousin Will.

"You bet he knows what's what," echoed Uncle Jim. "I had a presentiment that you'd have something good to fill us with when we got back, Brer."

"*We* let the deer slip too," cried Cousin Ross. "We were mighty nigh as empty as barrels, but we had no use for venison. Besides, we had no time to fool with such small game. We were after bear steak."

"Since we missed that, I'm willing to take what I can get. Give me another piece of that beef, if you please, Bud; it's mighty good."

"Where'd you learn to hunt deer anyway, Brer? I'd like to take lessons."

"'T isn't every one who would have pluck to fire at two eyes in the dark. Might think it was a ha'nt, you know."

"That's so. We old fellows might have been fools enough to wait and find out what the critter was, and would n't have a thing to show for our pains."

"You going to give the antlers to your sweetheart, sonny? What will you take for the hide?"

Brer had his reward for keeping his temper through all this chaffing nonsense.

"Brer's bound to go along when we go for that bear," said Cousin Will, as they pushed back their chairs from the table; "we can't spare such a fine hunter as he is."

"I reckon he might go along if his mother is willing," said Mr. Lee, smiling down into his son's eager face.

No one proposed that they should take Gene along. Usually everything was for "Brer and Gene;" but this time Gene's name was not so much as mentioned. It was almost enough to make him wish that he had been the one to blunder into shooting Lodi, since everybody made such a joke of it, and Brer was going to get such a treat for it. And so it might have been himself, instead of his brer, if Flo —

Gene caught his father's stern eye, and at once the tenor of his thoughts were changed. He realized that he had no cause to complain, but rather reason enough to be thankful that his shameful act was passed over in silence. He would have been still more thankful, had he known how his mother had pleaded with his father the night before to spare him the severe punishment that he deserved for his cruel deed.

"I think that Flo's suffering and his own shame will be sufficient punishment," Mrs. Lee had said.

"Well, I'll leave him to you. His mother knows how to manage the boy better than I do, I reckon. I certainly should make him smart for such meanness; but try your own way," Mr. Lee had finally conceded.

The hunters did not carry out their threat to settle down under the water-oaks until Lodi's fresh meat was consumed; but they lingered about the fireplace in the room, smoking their pipes, and telling over for the hundredth time the larks of their boyhood and the adventures during war times, to which exciting tales Brer and Gene never tired of listening. Neal, however, was all out of patience with them.

"Those old stories!" she exclaimed in disgust. "I should think they would wear out sometime. I've heard them so many times, I get them all mixed, so I don't know whether it was Cousin Will that chased a wild-cat without a gun, or Cousin Morris; and I'm sure I don't know which one it was that the Yankees did n't shoot, or the one that did n't kill the Yankees. I wish they'd hush and go home, so that Papa could find me another Nanny, like he promised."

"Perhaps he would n't find a Nanny if

he went," suggested Joy, as the only consolation that she could offer.

Neal truly had a trial of patience that day; for the sun had descended halfway to the western pine-tops before the hunters mounted their horses and rode off into the piney woods, shouting out promises, as they went, to return soon for the bear hunt.

"Of course Papa can't go now; it's so late," pouted Neal, "and all the stray lambs will be eaten up by the wild-cats and the bears!"

"You'd better take care of the Nanny you've got, instead of crying for another," suggested Gene. "I reckon she's hungry enough to eat the wild-cats and bears, from the way she's bleating."

Neal received this rebuke glumly; but she got the Nanny-bottle of milk and water, and went slowly to the orchard gate, where her lamb had been standing for the past half-hour, keeping up a continuous baa-baaing that was quite distracting.

"Hush, you baby!" cried Neal, crossly, when the lamb bounded frantically against her, almost upsetting her in its eagerness to reach the bottle. "You're not hungry. If you want to cry, *cry!* until you are tired. You're as tight as a barrel," poking the woolly sides; "you don't know when you've got enough! You behave so, I have a mind not to give you a bit. Get away!"

She held the bottle high over her head and ran lightly around the orchard; but Nanny bounded close to her, and finally tripped her down.

"There, take it, you greedy thing!" cried Neal, holding the bottle with both hands.

When it was half emptied, she pulled it sharply away; and jumping to her feet before Nanny had time to recover from her surprise, she ran nimbly across the orchard and slipped through the gate, slamming it quickly behind her.

"No; you sha'n't have another bit!" she

declared, facing about and addressing the lamb, who was attempting to squeeze into the crack and push the gate open.

"If you'd behave decent, and not butt me round so, you might have it all; but I'm tired of being knocked about by such a great strong thing as you, that's big enough, and ought to have sense enough, to eat grass. I'm going to hunt a little Nanny that's sure-enough hungry, and that has n't learned such rough manners as you, and won't push me down."

Having declared this sudden resolution, Neal marched smartly under the shade of the water-oaks and out of the opposite gate that opened on the road leading into the piney woods.

Her mother saw her trudging up the road with the bottle clasped close to her breast.

"Neal's gone to hunt a new Nanny," she said with a smile.

"I 'll trust her not to go far. She 's

too timid to venture into the piney woods
alone. There, she is stopping now," replied
Mr. Lee, who was standing on the gallery
beside his wife's chair.

But Neal had paused only for a moment,
to calculate her distance from home; and
seeing the Water-Oaks still quite near, she
flitted on and was soon hidden by the buck-
eye bushes.

She had caught the faint bleat of a young
lamb just over the little knoll before her;
and she sprang eagerly forward, hardly heed-
ing that she was entering the woods. What
matter if she were? they were almost as
open and full of sunlight as the clearing,
and the Water-Oaks were right behind.

She stopped on the brow of the hill and
looked before her with a pleased smile; for
there was the prettiest picture in the world.
A flock of a dozen or more sheep were
browsing through the sunny glade; while
in their midst a number of young lambs

were dancing and frolicking in the liveliest
fashion, leaping lightly over some large pine
logs that had been dashed down in a heap
by the wind, or prancing along the length of
the fallen trunks like kittens.

"Oh, you pretty Nannies! What fun!"
cried Neal, longing to join in their sport, and
going forward slowly, so that she would
not startle them. But as soon as they perceived her, the lambs dashed away to their
mammies, who lifted their heads and stared
wildly at Neal's strange little figure; and
then, suddenly wheeling about, they made a
dash over the opposite knoll, and with their
lambs close at their heels, they disappeared
from sight.

"You need n't be scared of me. I ain't
a bear," cried Neal, huffily, after them. But
at the word "bear," she bethought herself,
and looked anxiously around. It was not so
light down there in the hollow as it was on
the hill. Night was coming on. She reck-

oned that she had better go back and give the rest of the milk to her own Nan. She had better manners than these wild things, after all. Neal had run but a few steps, however, when she heard a faint pleading bleat behind her. Looking back, she spied a Nanny standing on the very spot whence the flock of sheep had disappeared.

"Ba-a, ba-a!" it called plaintively.

"Ba-a!" answered Neal, instinctively. But when she saw the little creature begin to trot eagerly toward her, she waved her apron and cried, "Shoo, shoo! Go back to your mammy, you little goose!" for she knew that she would be very severely blamed by her father if she enticed a lamb from the flock, and this lamb's mammy doubtless was with the other sheep in the next hollow; so she did her best to frighten the lamb away, and finally she turned and ran as fast as she could toward home. But the Nanny, having once recognized her voice as its mammy's, refused to give her up, and came briskly leaping along behind her.

"Go back!" screamed Neal, stopping at last and stamping her foot.

The lamb stopped too, but it refused to be turned back by her frantic efforts to wave it off; and when Neal started for home again, the lamb followed.

"I reckon I'm bound to take you back to your mammy!" exclaimed Neal, in despair. It was quite shadowy in the hollow now, but the sun still lighted up the woods on the opposite knoll very brightly. It would take her but a minute to run across and get rid of the Nanny, and then she could fly home in no time.

"Come on, then, you ninny!" she called; making a circle around the lamb, she ran down the slope into the hollow and panted up the opposite side, the lamb whisking along behind her.

Neal slackened her speed as she neared

the crest of the hill, not only because she was out of breath, but so that she should not frighten off the flock of silly sheep again. But where were they? She peered down into the shadowy glade in vain, for not a woolly coat was to be seen.

"I reckon I scared them so they 're running yet," thought Neal, laughing at the picture of the frightened sheep scurrying through the piney woods. "Well, I can't help it, even if they run clean off into Grandma's Bay. Come on, Nanny; I 'll give you some milk, and we 'll go home."

But as Neal advanced, the lamb retreated. "Come here, you silly thing! Ba-a, ba-a! Come and get some milk." She made a dash to seize it; but in sudden fright the lamb gave a whisk of its tail and bounded out of reach.

"Ba-a, ba-a!" coaxed Neal, advancing slowly and presenting the bottle. But the lamb had no knowledge of a bottle nor of its use, and again when Neal was putting forth her hand to grasp its wool, it scampered away.

" You have n't got a bit of sense," grumbled Neal, scrambling to her feet, for in missing the lamb, she had fallen prone on the pine-straw. She made an angry dash at the lamb, who scurried away as if it were beginning to enjoy the sport, bounding over pine logs and throwing out its long awkward, rag-baby legs in such a comical way as finally to overcome Neal's anger, and cause her to sink, exhausted and laughing, on the pine-straw; upon which the lamb wheeled around and gazed at her in innocent wonderment.

" I 'm laughing at you, if you want to know," explained Neal, becoming serious. " You look so funny and act so foolish. I never saw such a numskull. I 've got a lamb at home that has a heap more sense than you. She 's fond of me, and knows what 's good too; she just comes right up to me and takes all the milk I'll give her. I'm going right straight home to give her this, if you won't take it. I'll try you just this once. Ba-a, ba-a!"

Neal baaed in perfect mammy-like tones, and creeping gently forward, held out the bottle enticingly. The lamb, without a sign of fear, let her come within a hopeful distance; but just when she thought she surely should capture it, it had skipped over a log and was regarding her at a safe distance.

Neal was thoroughly out of patience.

"I'm going home, straight," she informed the lamb. "If you want to come, why come; perhaps Joy will have you, I won't."

She faced resolutely toward home; but after advancing a few paces, she glanced back over her shoulder to see if the lamb were following.

No, it was standing exactly where she had left it, and was not even watching her. That would never do. She could not leave that poor motherless thing out in the woods alone to starve.

"If you don't come, a bear will eat you," she cried, stopping. "Ba-a, ba-a, ba-a!"

The Nanny's attention was called back to her by the familiar mammy call; and when she moved forward again, it started to follow.

"That's right; hurry up. It's getting right dark," said Neal. She hastened briskly onward, keeping up the "ba-a, ba-a," that led the Nanny on.

The woods were quite gloomy by this time, for the sun had sunk down behind the trees. It was not pleasant at all to be out there in the dusk. She was not lost, — her face was turned directly toward home; but she had no idea that she had run so far in her wild chase of the Nanny. She was a decided little coward, as everybody knew, and she cast fearful glances about as she hurried along.

Things looked so strange in that half-light. Was that a man's head popping up from behind a fallen log? She knew that it was only a burnt stump, but she could not help running faster; but she stopped abruptly, for there, directly in her path, sat a darky with his dog on a log. She turned cold with fear, and a great lump in her throat seemed to be choking her, and then she sprang onward, trying to laugh. The darky and the dog were nothing but pine boughs and their shadows. They were only unreal people, such as she always fancied when she was trying to go to sleep in the dark. Still she could not help seeing them, nor being frightened by them, and trembling all over.

That certainly was a man with a knapsack, tramping through the hollow before her! There were two people watching him!

Nonsense! they were only shadows and stumps, she knew. She shut her eyes tightly a moment; and when she opened them again, the queer figures were gone. But yonder was a funny lady kneeling beside a stump, and a preacher standing over her. Neal wished devoutly that these last two were real people; but they were not real, they were only shadow people, like the others. All at once they disappeared. At the same moment Neal herself suddenly slipped out of sight. Where was she?

Certainly she did not know, for she did not dare to lift her face and look around to see. She had dropped down with a dreadful jar into somewhere, and she was lying in a little heap, too stunned and frightened to want to think or hear or see or anything.

Suppose it was the "jumping-off place" that she had heard her father and the boys talk about so much, and which she had missed seeing because she was looking back at the lady and the preacher. If she had jumped off, how ever was she to get home?

"Oh, *Mamma, Mam-ma!*" she screamed, terrified at the thought of never, never going back to the people under the water-oaks. But her own voice frightened her, and she shrank into silence, shaking with the sobs that she tried to stifle.

" Ba-a, ba-a ! "

" Why, Nanny, Nan, Nan ! " she cried joyfully, delighted by the familiar sound. She raised her head cautiously and peeped out between her fingers ; but it was all dark, and she quickly buried her face again, for she hated the dark.

But again sounded the tremulous " Ba-a, ba-a ! " followed by a hurried pattering of feet that seemed to be above her head.

" Ba-a, ba-a ! " answered Neal, softly, for a Nanny could not hurt any one.

At this there was a quick clatter of feet, and the bleating sounded close at hand and directly over her head. She started to her feet and looked up. There, right over her, was a circular opening, through which she could see soft fleecy clouds flushed by the sunset, and the feathery pine-tops waving against the evening sky. She gazed up in a dazed way for a few moments, and then in an instant she understood all about it. This was a sink-hole into which she had fallen; and that Nanny tramping about overhead was not her own loving Nan, but the silly little thing that had been following her through the woods, and which she had forgotten all about in her haste and fright.

She knew now just where she was; it was the hide-and-seek sink-hole. Joy and she had called it that ever since one day of last spring when, as they were running about picking the violets that blinked mistily up from the pine-straw on all sides, they had come unexpectedly upon this hole, and spied a cluster of sweet-marguerites hidden down there. A flood of light was pouring through the opening directly upon the flowers, and showed them, standing daintily on the very edge of a tiny stream that dimpled and sparkled about their stems for a moment and then went singing on — where?

The girls stretched themselves at full length on the pine-straw, and hung their heads far over to examine the home of the sweet-marguerites, and to see whence the water came and whither it went. They discovered that they were lying upon a thin crust of earth that covered a cavity of considerable depth and extent. Its sides and ceiling were rough and unsightly with loose soil and bristling roots. On opposite sides were the mouths of dark passages as high but not so broad as the marguerite-room; through these the water flowed in a shallow stream. When they kept perfectly still, the girls could hear it chattering and gurgling and whispering mysteriously far away under the dark earth.

This was one of the many underground streams that drain the hills and hollows of the piney woods. It had begun its course many long seasons ago, working its way at first slowly and laboriously under the clayey surface, root-bound and hard baked by the hot sun and the hotter forest fires that annually swept over it. Each rainfall that swelled its current helped to wear the channel deeper and broader, until now it could flow freely along a spacious passage, cool and dark, until at the end of its course it burst out into the sunshine and mingled with the swift current of Tyty Creek.

The opening through which the girls looked down was probably made by the hoof of a cow or of some other heavy animal, and had slowly enlarged by the crumbling of the soil from its edge.

The sweet-marguerites, poised lightly over the water on their slender stems, lifted their faces fearlessly to the children, who were shouting with delight at sight of the delicate lavender blooms, and reaching out longing hands toward them.

But the marguerites were quite safe in their underground home, for the little grasping fingers fluttered high above their heads; so they smiled sweetly at the girls until Neal and Joy concluded, very wisely, that they looked too lovely down there with their shadows fluttering on the water to be disturbed. It would be a shame to drag them from their chosen home; it was so cunning of the flowers to hide there.

When the girls had named it the "hide-and-seek hole," neither of them had thought of it as being a desirable hiding-place for any one but the marguerites and the happy little streamlet; so when Neal so unexpectedly found herself down there, although she was greatly relieved to know that she had not slipped over the "jumping-off place," and to know that she was not far from home, she was not rejoiced to find herself in the subterranean home of the marguerites.

The flowers of course were not yet up;

and fortunately the stream ran only during wet seasons, so now its bed was quite dry, else poor Neal would have been far more uncomfortable than she was, though it would have been difficult to make her think so.

She gave a wild spring and tried to clutch the edge of the opening with her hands; but though she was very light and agile, and she jumped with all her might until she was out of breath, she could not come anywhere near the opening.

"Ba-a, ba-a!" she called, to keep the Nanny from straying away.

She peered about in the vain hope of finding something on which to climb out. She looked up and down the deep black passages and shrank fearfully back from them. At last she managed to pull herself up the side of the cavern, by means of the tearing, scratching roots, to the roof, where she hung as long as her fingers would hold, while she tried to force her way out through the hard crust of earth and the network of roots, but this was impossible, and she dropped down, bruised and weeping.

The rosy flush had disappeared from the sky, and it was becoming quite dark up there in the piney woods.

"Nanny," she sobbed, "go home and tell them where I am."

The Nanny did not respond to this appeal, for it had wandered away, and she could hear its plaintive bleat, now here, and now there, as it sought its lost mammy.

"Ba-a-a, ba-a-a!" called Neal, as loudly as she could; and then she sank back against the side of the sink-hole, for suppose a bear should take her for a sheep.

The Nanny had heard her anyway, for she could hear it coming wearily this way, calling plaintively.

"I wish we were together," moaned Neal.

The lamb paused quite close to the hole.

Neal could just see its head turning uneasily against the sky. She could not help answering the lonely little creature.

Hardly had she done so when there was a plunge and a heavy fall almost into her lap.

"Nanny, Nanny!" she cried, folding her arms around the warm woolly little body. "Are you hurt? Are you killed?"

The Nanny's frightened struggles assured her that it was uninjured. She groped around in the dark for the Nanny-bottle, and after some struggles she managed to insert the nipple between the toothless gums of the unwilling lamb. After that, there was no further trouble; for having once tasted the milk, the Nanny drank it hungrily, and nestling down in Neal's arms, the weary little creature went comfortably to sleep.

Even a stupid Nanny is a great comfort sometimes. Neal forgot that it might be a bait for bears and wild-cats. It was a dear little thing, so trusting and innocent and warm. Neal curled around it; and, to keep herself from thinking of the dark, she tried to keep time with the breathing of the Nanny, but she soon forgot to do that, for she too dropped off to sleep.

She slept soundly for a number of hours; for when at last she started up to the strange consciousness that she was making the worst possible faces at somebody, she saw the round face of the moon looking fully down upon her. At first she thought it a part of her dream, — the strange opening above her and the pines waving up there in the moonlight; but when she tried to clasp Joy and felt the Nanny in her arms instead, she was quite wide awake.

It was very comforting to see the moon, for she and the man were very good friends, and had exchanged stares many a time, though they never had spoken. He looked especially mild, and gazed steadily down as if to assure her that he understood all about it and had come to keep her company; while the large star close beside him blinked and winked ceaselessly in the most knowing and encouraging manner.

"They'll be around soon," it seemed to say.

"Yes, morning will come pretty soon," Neal winked back bravely. It never occurred to her that any one would take the trouble to come out into the woods at night to search for her. She thought of everything as going on in the usual way at the Water-Oaks, as if her absence would make no difference.

"I wonder who's sleeping with little Joy," she thought; and she hugged the Nanny closer and buried her quivering face in its wool.

She wished that she would not keep thinking of those ghostly people that she had *not* seen out in the piney woods, and expecting them to come and peer down at her. As if piney-woods ghosts could walk or see, — especially when there were no such things!

She closed her eyes tight and tried to go to sleep, so that morning would come quickly; but just then the awful thought occurred to her that a snake might have made its winter home in the sink-hole.

Her hair seemed actually to be lifting from her head, she was so frightened; and though she knew there was no one to hear her, she could not help it, but gave the most dreadful scream, that sounded like nothing she had ever heard, and that terrified her even more than the thought of the snake had done.

The Nanny was frightened too, and springing up, began to dash blindly against the sides of the sink-hole, so that Neal had to forget her own fears in trying to quiet it. "Why, Nanny, poor thing, I did n't mean to frighten you. Here, Nanny, Nanny, come and lie down."

Suddenly the moonlight disappeared from the hole, and they were in utter darkness.

"Hullo, Nealie, so you done found your Nanny, did you?" spoke a familiar voice with a decided ring of joy in it.

"Oh, Gene, *is* that you? I'm *so* glad." Neal gave a sob of relief. "I ain't scared and I ain't lost; but I just fell into this horrid hole, and Nanny came tumbling after me, so I could n't get home."

"I should think not; but now I've found you, you're all right," he said protectingly. "Come on; I'll pull you out." He lay flat on the ground and stretched down his arms; Neal hoisted Nanny up just as far as she could, but with all his straining Gene could not quite reach her.

"Leave her, and you come; jump!" panted Gene.   "I'll get her afterward."

"You can't," objected Neal.

"Yes, I can. Come on."

Neal tried her best to reach those grasping hands; but she could not even touch the tips of the fingers. She sank down in despair.

"I'll wait for Papa," she faltered.

"No, you won't wait for Papa, as if I could n't get you out. Keep Nanny out of the way. I'm coming."

Before Neal could object, he dropped heavily down beside her. "Whew!" he exclaimed, "I did n't know it was that deep."

"Now we are all three here," cried Neal, half laughing and half crying.

"We won't be here long. Now, give me Nanny, and you just climb up to my shoulders like you used to on Papa's, and then you can boost Nanny out and jump after, just as easy as nothing."

It was not such an easy feat to perform as it was to talk about; but after some hard struggling and puffing, Nanny and Neal were both safely above ground. That was all very satisfactory, and Neal glanced around through the moonlit woods with a happy sigh; she would be all right as soon as Gene was up, to banish those horrid piney-woods spectres that her eyes *would* see.

But Gene did not come up. Neal could hear a great scratching and scrambling down there, but no Gene appeared. She peered down anxiously.

"Come on!" she called.

"How can I, I'd like to know?" cried Gene, crossly.

"I don't know. I thought you knew."

"How could I know this was as deep as a well?" demanded Gene.

"If there only was a bucket, I could draw you out."

"Yes, but there isn't a bucket, you see."

Gene, down below in the dark, set his wits to work to think up some means of escape, while Neal, above, looked fearfully around. She saw all sorts of queer things that she did not dare to mention to Gene, for fear he would call her a coward; but at last she saw something that she knew was no fancy. It was a blazing torch swaying above the brow of the knoll. It rose higher and higher, and presently a man's arm and head appeared; he was coming straight toward her.

She seized the Nanny, who was curled up against her, and dropped precipitately into the sink-hole.

Fortunately, Gene was not directly beneath the opening, or he might have been badly hurt; as it was, she knocked him with such force as to throw him against the rough sides of the hole and bruise him considerably.

"Good*ness!* What on earth —" he shouted in no gentle voice.

"Sh!" whispered Neal, clutching his arm fiercely. "Somebody 's coming!"

"Somebody — a shadow in your eye. *Ouch!* let go my arm!"

But Neal clung all the closer.

"No, it 's *some*body, with a torch."

"Papa and Brer! and *you*, bolting out of sight like this; and they out hunting you half the night! Holler for all you're worth!" and Gene lifted up his voice in a series of lusty shouts, while Neal screeched wildly. In a moment a pack of dogs was clustered around the hole, wagging their tails, and howling and barking in happy chorus. The light of a torch flashed down upon the children; and in another moment Neal, with her Nanny clutched close, was sobbing and laughing in her father's arms, while Gene was explaining, —

"I just could n't stay at home, Papa, when I thought of Neal out here getting scared to death at all the nothings she sees in the dark. I thought a ha'nt had her, sure, when I first heard her yell."

CHAPTER IV.

A STRANGE CROP.

THERE were some things about the sink-hole that neither Gene nor Neal had meant to tell; but somehow all came out, and they were well laughed at and teased.

But Neal was used to being made fun of, and did not mind it in the least; and Gene, having learned his lesson of self-control from his unhappy experience with Flo,—moreover, having seen his brer endure some pretty tough teasing with determined good-nature, — bit his lips and kept the old temper down right manfully.

He did insist, however, that he would have come up from the sink-hole all right by his own unaided efforts, if they only had given him time.

"I reckon you thought you 'd grow out," Brer remarked dryly.

Neal's wondering eyes opened wide at this suggestion, and she fell to pondering such a strange idea. She said nothing about it for the present, however; she waited a whole week, until the boys had gone off on the bear hunt with the hunters. For to Gene's inexpressible delight, he received, at the very last moment, permission to accompany his brer, Mr. and Mrs. Lee having decided, from seeing his determined efforts to control his temper, that he might again be intrusted with a gun.

Two faithful dogs were left to help Flo guard the house, so that Mrs. Lee and the girls and Nip, and black Nance in the kitchen, need have no fears during the hunters' absence.

When Brer and Gene rode off with the men, sitting erect and proud on Jinny and Nag, and trying not to grin from ear to ear with delight, the girls half wished that they were boys going on a hunt, — only they were afraid of bears. After all, they would much rather stay at home with their dolls — and Nip. They actually were to have Nip all to themselves, without danger of the boys coming in to interrupt and to make fun of their dolls.

Their dolls were a rather ridiculous set, to be sure, but they would have been much more respectable if the boys had let them alone; and in any condition they were very precious to the girls, who only wished that they had more.

All counted, there were five; but Elodia, the beautiful doll from New Orleans, with wonderful real hair, with eyes that closed, and with a pitiful little voice when she was punched sufficiently hard on the stomach, was usually laid carefully away in her box, so she only counted when she came forth in all her splendor on state occasions. Celia's china head was in Mamma's basket waiting for a new body. Beauty's rubber nose was worn off, and she had turned quite black with mortification; moreover, she was minus a leg and both arms, so that she was in no condition to be fussed over. Accordingly, there remained but one doll apiece for the girls to dress and whip and shake and hug and kiss.

Nip was much better than a doll, because he was alive. Dressed up in one of Mamma's cast-off gowns and an old bonnet, with his face well dusted with powder to give him a fair complexion, he made a very stylish lady indeed, poising his head jauntily and tripping about precisely like Aunty. He was charming company too, and the girls exchanged visits with him all the time.

"Why, Mrs. Nip, howdy. Come right in and sit down." Joy was keeping house on the north end of the gallery. "Here's Mrs. Neal staying with me while her husband's off on the hunt. Let me take your bonnet —oh, no, I forgot you must keep it on to cover the wool.— Ahem! Well, how is your sweet Beauty to-day?"

"Beauty doan feel right sma't dis mo'nin'. Her laig done git lame, case she dis'bey her maw an' go hoppin' roun' on it. She's right heavy, an' I done tole her one leg ain't 'nough to 'spo't her. She's mighty bad, an' I's 'bleege to keep her woun' up right tight in dis yer ole petticoat ob Joy's — oh, I mean dis yer boo'ful shawl from Grammer Bay, so she doan run 'way, an' git her 'plexion spoilt in de sun. She's jes' boun' to hab her own way, an' she gits away, case I's boun' to do som'fin else dan hol' on to her all de time. Dar she goes dis minute! Come yer, you to'mentin' chile; I's boun' to gib you a sma't w'ippin' fo' doin' me dat-a-way." For Beauty had suddenly thrown off her wrap, and made a flying leap over the side of the gallery.

Mrs. Nip rushed after her wilful child, and

brought her back, shaking her vigorously by her one arm.

"I's gwine to gib you a w'ippin' yo's boun' to 'member," exclaimed the tried mother, and suited the action to the word by laying poor Beauty across her knee and pounding her until she cried for mercy in Joy's voice, and said she would not do so any more.

"I's gwine put yo' whar yo' boun' to be safe, so I ken tak a li'l' comfo't a-visitin' wiv de ladies."

Having put Beauty into his chair and seated herself firmly upon her, Mrs. Nip brushed the anxious frown and some powder from her forehead, and resumed the conversation.

"W'at fo' yo'-alls cryin' dis boo'ful mo'nin'? Is yo' li'l' chilluns sick?"

Neal wiped the tears of merriment from her eyes and pursed up her mouth in a polite simper.

"Beulah is right well, thank you, Mrs.

Nip; but she gets so lonely playing all alone."

" Lily, too," chimed in Mrs. Joy.

" Oh, say, Nip," cried Neal, breaking in upon their play and the conversation quite impolitely, " how long would it have taken for me and Gene and Nanny to grow up out of the sink-hole, do you reckon ?"

Nip was obliged to meditate a few moments over this startling question.

"I reckon dat 'pend on de we'der," he said at last, with a twinkle in his eye. " Ef de rain come down right sma't an' doan wash yo'-alls 'way, I 'low how yo' boun' to show yo'self 'bove groun' bimeby."

" As long as the beans, do you reckon ?"

" I 'low yo'-alls doan wan' come up wrong-side-up, lak de beans does."

" Well, the beets, then ?"

" De beets boun' 'bide mostly undergroun'. You an' Gene an' de Nanny doan wan' do dat-a-way."

"No, of course not; but *do* you think we would be up by this time, Nip?"

Neal spoke very earnestly, and leaned so far forward in her rocking-chair that it slipped from under her and let her down upon the gallery floor; but she was just as comfortable there, and waited impatiently for an answer to her question.

"I reckon yo'-alls come up de day befo' to-morrer," answered Nip, rolling up his eyes wisely. "Case why, Neal? Yo' gwine to plant yo'self?"

"No, of course not; but I *do* want some more dolls. Say, Joy, let's plant Celia's head, and Beauty's arms and leg, and —"

Joy clapped her hands in delight.

"And Lily's loose eye," she screamed excitedly. "We'll just have heaps of dolls."

"Oh, hush, let's not tell until they're up," cautioned Neal. "Do you reckon it's good planting weather, Nip?"

"Fus-rate. I reckon it gwine rain dis ebnin'."

"Well, come on, then. Let's hustle. You get Celia. Here's the arms. Where's the leg?"

"In the churn in the store-room."

In a few minutes the children were hurrying with their queer seed to the corn-patch. Nip was armed with a spade, while Neal and Joy dragged one a rake and the other a hoe after them.

The cornfield had just been ploughed, and the clayey soil was sticky, but it was soft and easy to work, and, besides, no one was likely to come that way to spy their garden.

They chose the very farthest corner, and fell to work with a will. It was a large, smooth bed when it was made, and looked very inviting indeed.

In the northwest corner they planted Celia's head. It made them feel very sad to cover her up; but they left the round shiny top of her head above ground so she could grow out faster.

Lily's eye they covered entirely, like a seed, in the southwest corner, and marked the spot with three little sticks.

The two arms and leg they planted in the two remaining corners, pointing fingers and toes upward, since it was on the other ends that they needed to take root and grow.

"'Pears lak we's gwine hab a mighty small crap fo' sech a big bed," said Nip, suggestively. "I reckon dere's room fo' de whole ob Beauty in de middle."

"Oh, let's cut her up, like an Irish potato! She's no 'count, anyway. Won't it be fun to see the dolls popping up all over! You get her, Joy — and the scissors too. Me and Nip'll dig holes."

This bright idea was accordingly carried out. Poor Beauty was ruthlessly cut up, the bits planted in straight rows and smoothly covered over.

"Now, don't say a word to *any*body until they are up, and then no one will have a chance to make fun of us. Boys think girls have n't got any sense, but we 'll just show them! Don't you go and tell, Nip."

"I ain't gwine say a wo'd," Nip assured them, and went off to the barn with the tools, whistling nonchalantly, just as if nothing had happened.

The girls slipped quietly back to the gallery, and made great show of playing with their two remaining dolls, but they could not help blinking knowingly at each other and bursting into smothered giggles whenever they looked at Nip's preternaturally solemn face.

"My little daughters must have a very funny secret," Mamma remarked once, but she asked no questions to embarrass them.

Toward evening it began to rain, just as Nip had prophesied. It rained all night, but cleared in the morning. The girls sent Nip repeatedly to look at the corn-patch, and he reported every time that all was well.

The third day was dry and clear, but the boys and the hunters came home *with the bear*, and in the excitement Neal and Joy forgot all about the dolly-bed.

The hunters came riding up with great blowing of horns and loud hurrahs.

"They-alls done tree de b'ar," Nip announced promptly, but when they drew rein at the gate there was nothing at all to be seen in the fodder-wagon, — nothing but a great pile of pine-straw.

But yes! what was that great black thing dangling at the end of the wagon? Neal and Joy approached it cautiously; but Nip seized it boldly in his little brown hands and began pulling with all his might.

"Look out!" cried Cousin Will, sharply; "that big claw 'll grab you."

The girls sprang back; but Nip only grinned and felt the long claws with his fingers.

"Dis yer claw ain't gwine grab nobody no mo'," he chuckled.

It was no easy matter to drag the huge bear to the ground and carry him into the yard.

Neal clung to her mamma's skirts; but Joy, when she saw that it surely was dead, allowed herself to be perched on the shiny black side of the great creature.

But what fierce little eyes it had, and what a cruel mouth, full of long white teeth! Neal knew that she should dream about it.

The hunters had a great frolic skinning it and cutting it up, and they ended with a grand feast of bear-steak.

This time, when they gathered about the fire, there was a *new* story to tell; and even Neal, folded closely in her father's arms, did not tire of hearing it, and asked more questions than anybody else.

The boys' faces fairly beamed with proud happiness. They themselves had not killed the bear, to be sure; but what was better, their father had killed it, and at the very first shot too.

It had all happened in the neatest way. The hunters had heard that the bear was eating lambs from the flocks above the head of Fish River; and so instead of going into the swamp again, they decided to lie in wait for him near the spring.

They did not build a camp-fire at night for fear of frightening him off, so they had to go without coffee, and eat cold potato-biscuit and some corn-pone and cold bacon.

They had tied the horses back a little in a sapling thicket, and Mr. Lee had offered to guard them while the others watched for the bear. This was very generous of him, for very likely he would be too far off to have a shot at the bear, which the boys thought was not quite fair.

But of course they decided to stay with their father, so they wrapped themselves in their blankets and lay down near the tree to which old Nag was tethered.

They placed their guns close beside them, for they meant to keep their eyes wide open and to listen with all their ears for the least rustle, for they were as anxious as any one to have a shot at the bear.

They were very tired, however, and before they had lain there long, Gene's eyes became so painfully heavy that he let them close for just a moment's snooze; and when Brer heard him snoozing so comfortably, he could not resist the temptation to take just one wink of sleep also. But somehow, neither of them thought to waken until a sharp *bang* right over their heads startled them half out of their senses.

"Lie still!" their father commanded in a sharp, low voice. He was on one knee beside them, aiming his rifle over them. He did not fire again. The hunters came running up. Mr. Lee lowered his gun and told the boys that they might get up.

They were on their feet instantly; and there, only a few yards from them, lay the huge black monster.

On his way to his evening feast, the bear had discovered the sleeping boys, and had turned aside to see what they might be.

Mr. Lee was just dozing off, when he was roused by Nag's plunging and snorting; and raising his gun, he had sent a bullet to the bear's heart just in time to save the boys from a crushing hug.

"Dat b'ar ain't got no sense ef he 'lowed you-uns was lambs," exclaimed Nip, scornfully.

"I think I must keep my boys with me next time," said Mrs. Lee.

The boys raised woful voices at this, but their father silenced them.

"Don't make me sorry I took you once, boys. Your mother will decide what is best when the next time comes."

No wonder that their planting was quite

driven from the girls' heads. Nearly a week passed before they thought anything about it, and then it was a remark of Brer's that recalled the dolly-bed to their minds.

"Did you plant some collards out in the corn-patch, Papa?" he asked one day at the dinner-table. He winked at Gene as he put the question, but the girls did not see that.

"Collards in the corn-patch! Certainly not."

"Well, *something* is coming up there, out in the far corner, close to the fence. The things did n't look like collards, they were so bright, but I did n't reckon anybody 'd make a flower-bed away out yonder. I 'm bound to see what they are this evening."

Neal nearly choked herself, she crammed her mouth so full of light bread, and Joy clutched her chair with all her might, and her face grew alarmingly red. But no one seemed to notice the girls; and they managed, by desperate efforts, to sit still until dinner was over.

When they left the table Neal was obliged to feed her two Nannies, and by that time the boys had called Nip off with them, so the two little girls had to go to the corn-patch without him. They caught a first glimpse of the dolly-bed from the top of the rail-fence, when they scrambled over.

"Oh, look, they're all dressed up!" screamed Joy, clasping her hands rapturously. "Don't they look fine!"

And in fact, the dolly-bed appeared to be blooming with figures that nodded and beckoned in the bright sunlight.

The girls stumbled breathlessly across the ploughed ground, never stopping, and hardly daring to look until they were quite close to the bed.

Then they clasped each other's hands and gazed wonderingly at their blossoming dolly-bed.

There was no doubt of it, they were actual dolls, though very curious ones, not in the least like the seed they had planted or the dolls in the house.

"They look like they had growed up from kernels of corn," said Joy, hardly daring to speak above a whisper lest the strange dollies should vanish.

"That's because they grew in the corn-patch," explained Neal, stooping down and lightly touching the one in Celia's corner.

"This don't look like Celia, but it's a doll."

"Yes, they're all dolls," said Joy, "and corn too, 'pears like."

No wonder that the children were puzzled. The group of dollies seemed to be made up entirely of corn-husks, — faces, arms, bodies, and all; only their dresses were of all the colors of Easter eggs.

"Let's pick them and take them in to Mamma," suggested Neal.

But just at this moment the boys and Nip sprang up on the fence close beside them.

"Oh, Nip, just see what's sprouting up!" cried Neal. "We just planted these dolls ourselves; Nip saw us," she declared to the boys, who were lifting their hands with "ohs" and "ahs" of amazement.

"I 'low Celia an' Beauty done growed up into co'n-dolls," was Nip's only remark, as he examined the wind-tossed blossoms.

"Gee, what a fine bouquet they'll make!" cried Brer. "Ain't you going to tote them to the house?"

"Of course we are. How do you pick them?"

"Oh, easy enough." Brer deftly pulled up the corn-stalk upon which one of the dolls grew.

The girls fell eagerly to work; and in a few minutes all the dolls were plucked and gathered in great clusters into their arms.

Neal lingered a moment to poke about in the dust, to make sure there were no traces of Beauty and Celia, but not an eye nor an arm could she find.

Mamma expressed as great wonderment as the boys had shown, at sight of the strange crop.

"I'm going to ask Papa to sow dolls in all the patches, and raise heaps of them for Santa Claus," cried Joy, ranging her armful in a fluttering row against the house along the gallery floor.

"Turnip-dolls, an' wata-melon-dolls, an' potato-dolls, an' cabbage-dolls." Nip began to tell them off soberly on his fingers; but at the idea of such ridiculous dolls Mamma and the boys went off into spasms of laughter, and finally Nip himself turned a summer-sault to hide a grin.

But Neal saw him smile, and it set her to wondering about those corn-dolls. She did not tell Joy that she suspected the boys of playing a trick upon them, but she refused to plant any more dolls. A long time after, when she had almost forgotten about the dolly-bed, she discovered Celia's clayey head stowed away in the far corner of the lowest drawer of the great bureau in the store-house. Then she knew.

CHAPTER V.

THE TRAMP.

As there is neither snow nor ice to melt away under the water-oaks, it is not always easy, unless one happens to have a calendar, to know just when spring has come.

But Nip and the children always knew, for in spring the johnnies came clustering up in dancing, daisy-faced crowds. The violets pushed through the pine-straw; the sweet waxy arbutus-flowers peeped, fresh and dewy, from beneath their coverlet of black-jack leaves; the buck-eye bushes turned red with heavy blooms; the swelling buds of the honeysuckle burst into fragrant pink clusters; the old-man's beard turned white and trailed its drooping branches in the sparkling waters of Sweet-Water Branch;

every laurel-bush was a huge, blushing bouquet; the tyty trees hung out dainty tassels
of the most delicate perfume, to tempt the
children and the bees; the yellow jasmine
trailed over the ground in luxuriant growth,
or climbed the slender saplings, bending
them low with the heavy weight of golden
fragrant blooms. Of course not all these
flowers came at once; that would be too
bewildering. They were expected to come in
proper order as the sun called them forth;
but they crowded upon one another in rapid
succession, or played truant, as the season
happened to suit them. The sweet bay came
more leisurely, also the creamy magnolias,
high up among the glossy leaves of the white-
trunked trees. These were the wild-flowers
flourishing in the hollows and hillsides of
the piney woods, and overhanging the
springs and branches.

In the clearing the peach-blooms were the
first and sweetest that came.

The whole peach orchard was a misty, rosy cloud dropping showers of dainty pink petals.

Sometimes a warm sun would coax the trees into bloom too early in the season; and Mr. Lee would be obliged to protect the tender buds from being nipped in a cold snap, by building a smudging fire in the orchard, so that the smoke could rise all through the branches and keep the frosts away. But frequently he was spared this trouble by the forest fires from which the smoke rolled in heavy waves through the piney woods.

The times when the woods were burning were very uncomfortable ones for Neal and Joy. Everything looked so strange in the smoky air; the sun seemed so low and red and hot as it rolled overhead; and the pine wall that bordered the clearing was so far away and misty; besides, they were always so thirsty and their eyes smarted so painfully. They had such a queer feeling, as if something dreadful were about to happen; they could not help expecting to see the fire every minute, though they knew it might be miles away.

Still, it always came at last, and their father and the boys had to fight it, and sometimes Mamma and old Aunt Nance.

How the fire started in the woods, no one ever knew; and a fine was claimed by government from any one who should light the dry grass, but still the fire came every year as surely as the springtime. Some said that lighted matches were dropped into the grass by lawless darkies who bore a grudge against the white folks, and wanted to burn them out of their comfortable homes; but nobody could prove that.

In former days, when the grass was thick and as tall as a man's head, the men who tapped the pine-trees for turpentine, and worked in the resin distilleries, used to set it afire to "run out the snakes;" but now that the grass was comparatively low, and the trees were bled of their sap, and the men all gone, there was no need of the burning, and it did much more harm than good. Government had even offered a reward to any one who should detect a person in the act of starting a fire. The boys had no such dread of the fire as Neal and Joy; they enjoyed the fun and excitement of "outing" it.

Mr. Lee always protected his home by ploughing around the outer fence of the patches, and causing the boys to rake away the dry grass and pine-straw.

He did so a little earlier than usual this year, because he was obliged to take a trip through the piney woods and across Grandma's Bay, to buy in town a supply of seeds, hominy, sugar, and such things as did not grow in the patches around the Water-Oaks.

He had not the least idea that the fire would come up for several weeks, though the woods were full of smoke; but he felt better to have the place protected.

"It is possible that I shall be kept till to-morrow," he called back, as he drove off behind Pacer early one morning; "but I *reckon* I'll be back to-night. Take care of your mother and sisters, boys, and don't let the trough and the critters go dry."

The boys were quite accustomed to being left in charge of the place, not only when their father went to town, or was off on a hunt, but during the long days that he spent alone in the woods riding over the sheep ranges.

"We'll have to work right sharp to finish it to-day," said Brer, leading the way to the barn as soon as their father was out of sight.

"We're just bound to finish it," exclaimed Gene, enthusiastically.

"We's gwine kotch de ole red sun on a pine-top an' holt him up, ef he wan' go to roost wiv de chickins, case we're boun' finish dat playhouse befo' night," Nip declared, in his turn, with an emphatic shake of his woolly head.

"Well, you and Nip feed the shotes and let out the calves, while I draw water. I reckon we'll be done by breakfast-time, and then we'll have all day. Lucky Papa let us off the milking, ain't it?"

The boys usually enjoyed a sort of holiday when their father was away, for work was his motto, and he meant to teach it to his boys early.

To-day, however, the boys had generously devoted to building a playhouse for Neal and Joy.

The girls were overjoyed and humbly grateful for this act of condescension in the boys; and their delight was not in the least dimmed by Brer's ungracious manner of proffering the favor.

"I reckon we're bound to build a house for these everlasting dolls," he had cried, giving Lily a contemptuous toss, "else we 'll have to sit off on the water-oak roots, the gallery 's so cluttered up."

"Oh, Brer, will you, with a window and a door and a table — ?"

"And a pianer and a sideboard — and — and —" mocked Brer. "I said a *house*."

"Well, make it under the cedar-tree, won't you, Brer?"

"I did n't say I 'd make it, did I? Now, hush; supposen we should, though, would you promise to keep all these corn-flowers there, and all the rest of this trash?"

"Yes; every*thing*. But if you won't make a door, how can we get them in?"

"Who said we *would n't* make a door? I declare, you make me right mad."

"I won't say another word; only, Brer, how can we see without a window?"

"Run and get that old window-sash from the barn, and look through it if you want to see."

Fortunately, the girls understood Brer perfectly, for there was always a good-natured ring in his voice and a roguish twinkle in his eye, however sharp his words might be.

As for the playhouse, the boys anticipated making it with as much eagerness and pleasure as the girls would enjoy seeing them do it.

They hastened with their morning's work; and when breakfast was over, and Brer had thrown out their corn-bread to the pack of dogs, they shouldered their axes and marched off to the pond, for the first thing to be done was to fell some saplings from the thicket and cut them into proper lengths, for the house was to be of logs, like the smokehouse, the storehouse, and the potato-house.

"We're coming too," shouted Joy, as she and Neal came trotting after, each with a doll tucked under her arm.

"Won't you bother and ask questions and jabber all the time?"

"No, we won't say a word. We'll be just as quiet as mice."

"All right, then; mind you keep out of the way when the trees fall. Better stay where you are."

Accordingly, the girls sank down on the pine-straw, and talked and planned rapturously of the new house and the pretty things with which they would furnish it. Every now and then a sapling crashed down; and the boys cheered as if it were the biggest tree in the forest. The girls, however, were too engrossed in their own plans to pay much attention to the boys, until they were startled half out of their wits by the most awful yelling, all three boys screaming at the tops of their voices. The girls jumped to their feet and stood staring wildly around, uncertain which way to run, for of course their first thought was, a bear.

But, no, the boys were pounding something on the ground. It must be a snake; only the boys never were afraid of snakes.

"We've done killed it," shouted Gene, at last. So the girls advanced cautiously.

Brer was sitting on a log, looking white and frightened; Gene was shaking as if he had a chill; while Nip was holding up a monstrous wiggling body of a snake on a stick.

"Dis yer snake ain't no moccasin," he said positively.

"It isn't a rattler either, nor a coachwhip, nor anything that I ever saw before," cried Gene, whose teeth were still chattering.

"It's a snake, anyway, that's sure, and the biggest one I ever saw," said Brer, trying to rouse from his fright. "I never knew a snake to do any one that-a-way before. Gee, how he squirmed!"

They had been working away merrily, planning to erect a house with all the modern improvements of which they knew; and Brer, having selected a fine straight sapling, pushed back into a buckeye bush to make room for a good sweep of his axe, when his bare foot had come down upon the cold, shiny coil of a squirming snake. Before he could move, the snake had lifted its head almost to a level with Brer's waist, and, striking, had seized the lappets of his pocket in its jaws.

Then it was that Brer, thinking that he was bitten, yelled in terror; and Gene, seeing the monster, had cried out too, Nip swelling the chorus with such vehemence that the startled reptile had dropped to the ground, and glided directly toward the spot where the girls were sitting. But in a twinkling, Nip had brought down his axe on the creature's struggling body, and had pinned it there until the boys had beaten out its loathsome life.

"Bring the ugly thing in and show it to Mamma. She'll be scared half to death when we tell her," cried Neal.

"We ain't a-going to tell her, nor you

either, until we've got our logs. You're willing enough to go in now, I reckon; but if you say a word about this before we come, you're bound not to get any house. Mamma would fancy the pond alive with snakes, and wouldn't let us cut another sapling. Go along in, but don't you say a word. We'll bring it and tell when we come." Brer had entirely recovered from his fright, and was himself again.

Except for this short interruption, the log-cutting went on smoothly all the morning, and in the afternoon the even, round lengths were fashioned rapidly into a fine square house.

Doubtless they would have completed it, door, window, and all, without any need of impaling the red sun on a pine-top to keep him from going down into the smoke and gloom of the forest, if a sudden, furious commotion among the dogs had not called them in haste to the front gate.

Some one was there, — a man quietly waiting a few yards back from the paling against which the dogs were savagely leaping.

"Go and speak to him, Brer," said Mrs. Lee, who had come out on the gallery.

Brer assumed his father's dignified bearing, and advanced to the gate.

"Howdy, Bud!" said the stranger, nodding familiarly.

"Howdy," Brer responded courteously, trying vainly to hush the dogs.

The stranger came a few paces nearer, so that he could make himself heard above the fierce barking.

"I'd like to speak a word with your father, Bud. He's somewhere abouts the clearin', I reckon."

"No, he's in town." This was a very indiscreet reply; and Brer bit his lip in vexation the moment he had made it. It would have been better, perhaps, to let such a rough-looking stranger think that there was some man about; but it was too late for that now.

"Gone for supplies, I reckon. I hope he 'll bring some tobac'; I 'm just out. Well, I suppose I can see your mother; I 'd like some grub and a night 's lodgin', if you can take me in."

Brer withdrew to consult his mother.

" Mamma will send you out a good meal, but she can't lodge you to-night. There 's another place about three miles ahead that you can reach before dark — "

" Oh, that 's too far; I can hardly limp now. Suppose you tie those dogs, and I 'll come in and talk with your mother. I reckon you don't have much company in this wilderness, and I 'low she 'd like to hear the news."

But Brer made no movement toward obeying his suggestion.

" Well, then, Bud, if you 're too lazy to tie them dogs, just call them off, and I 'll walk right in. I ain't afeared."

He walked boldly up to the gate.

"You'd better not," said Brer, quietly; "I might not be able to manage the dogs." And the angry animals made such a savage spring at him that the man withdrew rather hastily.

Gene came out with a plate loaded with corn-bread, sweet potatoes, bacon, and cold biscuit, with a foaming mug of corn-beer to wash it down.

The man received them over the fence, muttering angrily, "So your mother expects me to sit out here on a log, and eat cold grub, like a nigger."

"It is the best that we can do for you," answered Brer, with heightening color. "Those victuals are exactly what we all eat. If you don't want them, just hand them back."

"No you don't, sonny. Don't get riled. This corn-beer is n't bad; only I wish it was somethin' stronger. I 'll put this grub into my pockets, so I can chew on it if my shoe-leather gives out. There's a heap o' nourishment in cow-hide, you better b'lieve; that's why my shoes look so chawed up. I'm prospectin' through these parts with a view to takin' up a homestead, an' settlin' down with my fambly. Your house is the first I've come across in two weeks. I reckon I'll settle somewhere about here and be your neighbor. I'm a right social party, and thankful, too, for all favors. You just depend on't I won't forget you and your stale grub."

He cast a sharp, scowling look about the place, and slouched heavily up the road, turning once to shake his fist at the dogs, who kept up their fierce din as long as he was in sight.

"That's the meanest-looking man I ever saw," exclaimed Gene; "I'd just like to let the dogs out on him."

"You don't mean that, my son. I am always too sorry for such poor homeless men to be angry at their want of gratitude. Probably," Mamma added significantly, "he did n't learn to control his temper in his youth."

"But what is he going to do to us, Mamma?" wailed Neal; "he looked so mad."

"The man is n't going to hurt us, my child. Don't be foolish. See, he has gone quite out of sight."

"Dat man ain't gwine fur befo' he lose his whiskers. Mighty cur'us 'bout dose whiskers; dey des look lak dey gwine drap clean off when he talk so peart."

"Is that so, Nip? Were his whiskers really loose?"

"Dat's de truf, Brer; I seed him clap 'em on right sma't w'en he tuk notice how dey was a-slippin' down."

"I suppose he is some criminal or escaped convict," said Mrs. Lee; "but never mind, he's gone, and Papa will be here soon, so hurry about the work."

So it came about that the boys did not finish the playhouse that day.

"We-alls done fo'get to cotch de sun fo' he out ob reach," exclaimed Nip, regretfully, when the chores were done and the boys returned to the house.

"Oh, well, never mind. I'm tired enough, and the girls will just have to wait for their house;" and Brer threw himself wearily on the sheep-skin before the hearth, for a little fire in the evening was very cheerful and not at all uncomfortable.

Mrs. Lee sat in her cosey chimney-corner, watching the flickering blaze; while Neal and Joy nestled at her feet, prattling their sweet nonsense in soft undertone.

"Nip," called Mamma, presently, lifting her head to listen, "is n't that the wagon coming?"

"I reckon de wagin ain't comin', Miss Lyla; but me an' Gene 'low we-uns see a cur'us fiah a-bu'nin' yonda," answered Nip from the gallery.

"It's a sure light, Mamma," cried Gene.

Brer was on the gallery in a second, and Mrs. Lee and the girls hurriedly followed.

"Jes' put yo' haid yer, Brer, an' I reckon yo' 'll spy it 'tween de co'ner ob de Owlets' Roost an' de fig-tree."

"Yes, I see it, sure enough, Mamma. It's over the ridge, flaring up right in one spot. Now it's gone; no, there it is, brighter than ever. Somebody must just be starting it. You look right there through the fork of the fig-tree. Do you see?" Brer placed his mother carefully and pointed out the direction.

"Yes; but it appears to me more like a camp-fire than anything else. It does n't spread in the least. It's smothered and smoking now, as if fresh wood had just been thrown on. I reckon it is our tramp, camping out there for the night."

"But he's bound to set the woods a-fire or

do some mischief. Let me and Gene and Nip slip out and watch him."

"I hardly think there is need of that," objected Mrs. Lee. "Papa will be here presently. He will see about it. You don't want to deprive the man of such poor comfort as he can get from a pine-straw bed, do you?"

"No, of course not. Only I believe he's staying around for some mischief. Why, he's had time to tramp three or four miles since he left. He's just got *some* reason for hanging around, I know."

"Only let us go and peek at him, Mamma. He'll never see us," Gene pleaded. "We'll take Lyon along."

"Oh, no, it never would do to take a dog along. Lyon would tear him all to pieces. You must leave the dogs here, and you must promise me not to do anything rash. Brer, I trust to your judgment. If the man is only resting quietly, come away without disturbing him. If you see anything to make you think that he means mischief, send Nip back to report, and I 'll tell you what you had better do."

"All right, Mamma; we 'll be sensible. Had n't we better leave one of the guns with you ? "

"Leave both; you won't need them. You are better off without them."

"It would n't do any harm to take my gun. It 's only loaded with bird-shot. It might be a mighty good thing to have along if I wanted to scare him, you know."

"Well, take it, but remember what I say; keep quiet and don't rouse him. He is a desperate man, and it won't take much to make him angry."

It was not every day that there was a chance for such a jolly lark, and the boys stole off into the dark woods with the most rapturous feeling of adventure, which stirred all the more keenly in their breasts because it was mixed with uncertainty and the least bit of fear.

They soon reached the crest of the slope, where they could look down into the hollow and see the flames from which the light arose.

It was, as their mamma had said, a camp-fire. At first the flickering flames and the column of smoke were all that they could distinguish, because of intervening sapling thickets, the large pine stems, and fallen timber; but as they stole nearer, flitting noiselessly from tree to tree, they saw a dark figure pass between them and the light. They paused and waited breathlessly for it to reappear; but there was no further sign of life save a sudden burst of sparks, as if fresh fuel had been tossed upon the fire.

"If we can just creep down behind that pile of logs, we can see, easy, just what he is up to," whispered Brer. "Go right still, now. If he's by the fire, he can't see us; but if he's prowling round through the woods, he 'll be mighty apt to catch sight of us. Come on ; stoop low."

They glided quickly and quietly over the pine-straw until they were hidden in the shadow of the great fallen trees that had been twisted off and thrown together by fierce winds.

The boys were almost startled to discover how near they had approached the fire. Its light flickered brightly on the trunks of the pine-trees just behind them.

" Keep down in the shadow," Brer cautioned. They took off their hats and peeped warily over the logs. The first thing that their eyes rested upon was the figure of a man sitting with his feet to the fire and with his back propped comfortably against a pine-tree. As his face was turned toward them, and the warm light of the fire played brightly over it, they had a capital view of him. That it was not their tramp was the first thought of Brer and Gene. The tramp was a rough, hairy man; but this man's face, and head too, were quite bare, as they plainly could see, for he had tossed his hat aside.

Nip's sight was keener than the boys'. He crawled close to Brer and breathed into his ear, —

"I 'low he keep dem fine w'iskers and ha'r to dress up w'en he go visitin'."

Brer looked at the man sharply. His clothing certainly was exactly like that worn by the tramp, — dirty jean trousers, a buttonless torn coat of a yellow-brown hue tied together in front by a wisp of pine-straw, and a faded red kerchief knotted about his neck. And when one came to examine him closely, there was the same scowling face and angry eyes, more savage and repulsive than ever, now that the partial screen of hair and beard was removed.

He had been sitting perfectly still, with his hands clasped behind his head, and his eyes fixed steadily on the fire.

Presently, however, he started up with an impatient oath, and glanced suspiciously about him in the darkness. He seemed satisfied that there was nothing about, for having tossed two or three pine-burrs upon the fire, he settled down with his chin in his hands, and began muttering indistinctly to himself.

It sounded exactly like the growling of a bear, and an angry one at that. Once he lifted his head and looked with an ugly leer in the direction of the Water-Oaks; and he raised his fist and shook it threateningly.

"If he was a sure enough bear, and I only had a gun —" Gene began resentfully; but Brer's elbow gave his ribs an imperative nudge.

The tramp had sprung hastily to his feet, staring about with an expression of alarm on his face. He stood there but the briefest instant; then, with a quick movement, he scattered the blazing embers and disappeared behind the tree against which he had been leaning.

The boys crouched lower, but kept vigilant watch; and presently, by the light of the blazing pine-straw that the scattered fire had kindled, they saw a dark form skulking away into the dark woods.

"What did you go and scare him off for, you simpleton?" demanded Brer, in an angry whisper. "Did n't I tell you to keep still?"

"He made me that mad I 'd like to have hollered right out," muttered Gene, defiantly. "Who cares if he is gone? I don't, sure. The farther, the better."

"Yes, if he has gone. *Look behind you!*"

At Brer's admonition Gene whirled about, instinctively doubling his fists and falling into a posture of defence.

Brer laughed, "You 're fooled mighty easy."

Gene turned sharply upon his teasing

brer; but Nip's mild voice interrupted the explosion.

"Gwine let the woods burn out to-night, Brer?" he inquired in a tone of placid indifference.

"No, not if I can help it. Whew! how that fire is spreading! Get pine-tops, quick!"

He set the example by running forward, and, having placed his beloved gun against a tree, by seizing upon a young sapling, and deftly twisting and breaking its stem. With this fine broom for "outing" the fire, he rushed forward, shouting to the others to follow, and vigorously fell to beating the flames that were spreading nimbly over the pine-straw, forming two lines of fire burning rapidly in opposite directions, and running out longer and longer at the ends.

But he was hardly well at work, thrashing vigorously on this side and that, when he was interrupted by a wild yell from Gene.

"Drop that gun!" was Gene's cry.

"Well, no, young un, I ain't a-goin' to drop this fine gun just yet. It might go off and hurt somebody, you know."

Brer recognized the sarcastic voice of the tramp on the instant, and understood at once that he had stolen up in the darkness and gained possession of the rifle. He dropped his pine-top and bounded to Gene's assistance.

"Drop it, I tell you!" Gene was advancing fiercely upon the man, his face white with passion, and his fists raised threateningly.

The man laughed mockingly, and raising the gun, took quick aim at the advancing boy.

"Halt!" he commanded curtly.

Gene was too blinded with indignation and anger to pay the least heed; but Brer, cooler-headed and more sensible, saw the reckless gleam in the man's eyes, and he shouted imperiously, "*Stop, you Gene!*" and Gene stopped.

"That's right," said the tramp, lowering the rifle; "I s'h'd hate to see you hurt yourself, and you might run against a bullet, you know."

"You might run against one yourself, if you don't put down that gun. That's my brer's."

"Your brer's, is it? I 'lowed it was mine. If your brer wants to set up a claim for this fine new rifle of mine, he can speak out for himself; but he had better bide right where he is."

With this he turned the rifle upon Brer, who was slyly sidling toward him.

As Brer wisely obeyed him, and both boys stood at bay before him, the tramp lowered the gun, but held it in readiness for instant use.

The boys glared at him angrily, only waiting for a chance to spring; and he returned their gaze with an alert, angry expression, over which played a taunting smile that was very exasperating.

"So your ma sent you skulkin' out here in the woods to spy on me, did she? She was n't satisfied to turn me off like a nigger, but she had to send you to rout me out of a poor pine-straw bed. Your ma ain't no lady, she ain't. You may tell her so for me — if you ever see her again."

The brown eyes and the blue flashed threateningly.

"You'd better take care what you say about my mother!" said Brer, in a low, stern tone.

"My mamma is the best lady in the world!" shouted Gene, the veins swelling on his forehead.

Both boys were touched to the quick by this insult to their mother; and they were quivering to spring forward to avenge it. But the man was handling the gun significantly; and they restrained themselves.

"You 're right plucky little chaps, sure, to show fight to a great feller like me, what owns a fine new gun like this un. But I reckon me and my rifle are a match for a dozen of you and all your niggers. Where's that little darky hid himself?"

He spoke with some anxiety, and cast his restless gaze hither and thither through the woods, which were all alight now and flickering with shadows from the fire, that was roaring and leaping in triumphant glee. "It's time for me to be movin' on," he said; "it's gettin' too hot for me here. Look a-here, do you know what they do with spies?"

"Hang them," answered Brer, promptly.

"Or shoot them. Shootin''s the easiest and quickest. I've half a mind to let you off this time; but that's what I'm goin' to do to you if you don't turn those pockets of yours wrong-side-out this minute. Look sharp, now! You first!" He pointed the rifle squarely at Brer. But Brer thrust his hands solidly into his pockets and never flinched.

"Instantly the boys were upon him." — *Page* 187.

"Look sharp, I say!" shouted the man, angrily. "I'll give you while I count three, then you're done for, sure. Now, one — two — *three!*" the gun went off with a bang and flash; the man, with a smothered oath, threw up his hands and fell struggling backward. Instantly the boys were upon him. Nip, who came butting like a ram between the man's knees, was holding down the shorn head; Brer, heavily astride the prostrate body, struggled desperately, with Gene's help, to keep possession of the knotted hands that strained and wrenched with alarming strength.

"Let his head go, and get the gun," panted Brer, who felt that this was the only chance of conquering their desperate enemy. "Have you fixed it? Cock it, then, and just give it to him if he budges."

The whites of Nip's eyes showed diabolically in the firelight. He took aim at the man as if he would like nothing better than to touch the trigger. The man looked up the glistening length of the barrel and was quiet.

"Do just what I told you," repeated Brer, in cold, measured tones. "If he stirs, shoot. Now, Gene, just let go his hands; we won't bother ourselves to hold him." He arose deliberately from his seat on the man's chest and drew some stout cord and a knife from his pocket. "Turn on your face!" he commanded.

"You told me not to stir," retorted the man.

"But now I tell you to stir, and you'd better mind! Nip, if he does n't do as I tell him, you just let him have it. Now turn!"

Brer's voice quivered ever so slightly as he said this, for the man's face was becoming terrible in its wrath; and Brer knew, and Gene knew, and Nip knew, that there was not a single loaded cartridge left in the barrel; and if the man had one suspicion of this, he would spring to his feet and dash upon them. They were not strong enough to hold him, and the empty gun was their only chance of victory.

Slight as it was, the prisoner caught that uncertain tone in Brer's voice, and a shrewd gleam lighted his sullen eye. He made a show of obeying, and turned ever so slightly; then he paused and asked,—

"What for do you want me to turn?"

"Never mind what for. You just turn."

The man moved slightly over, bringing his right hand around to the ground; and Brer noticed with alarm that he was slowly drawing up his foot.

"Turn, I say!" shouted Brer.

But, quick as a flash, the man drew himself together for a spring, when —

"*Turn!*" thundered a stern voice, and a rifle was thrust close to the wicked face.

The man dropped and rolled over.

"Now tie him, Brer," said Mr. Lee, quietly.

"Here, Nip, take my gun, — it 's good for three or four bears, — and if he does n't mind on the instant, just blow his brains out. Brer, march him home and lock him into the potato-house. Leave the rifle with your mother; she 'll look out for him, and you and Nip come back here. Gene, get your pine-top and come with me; this fire will get away with us if we don't look sharp. There 's a tree caught, already. I must stop that. You begin at this near end. I 'll be with you in a minute."

Brer had no further trouble in managing the tramp. Having securely tied his hands behind his back, he helped him to stagger to his feet, and pointing toward the Water-Oaks, bade him, " March ! " The man obeyed sullenly. From the moment when he knew that escape was hopeless, he never but once opened his lips to utter a word while they had him in charge.

Brer followed him closely, with cocked

gun, while Nip led the way, carrying the man's hat, and ragged wig and beard.

When they reached the Water-Oaks and entered the yard, it required all Brer's authority to hold the dogs in check, to keep them from springing upon the man and tearing him to pieces; and when he was safely lodged in the potato-house, they dashed in howling, barking circles around it. Before locking him in for the night, Brer caused Nip to cut the cords that bound his hands and to spread on the ground a pallet that Mrs. Lee had provided.

The prize was safe till morning; and Brer and Nip bounded like deer back to the woods, where the fire was making alarming headway.

Mr. Lee, however, was an experienced fire-fighter. When he saw that the rushing wave of fire had become too fierce to be beaten out with pine-tops, he took a lighted brand, and drawing it through the pine-straw some rods in front of the advancing flames, he kindled a counter line of fire, which, seizing eagerly upon the intervening pine-straw and grass, and drawn in by the fierce upward draught caused by the intense heat of both fires, rushed to meet the advancing sheet of flame; and in a few moments the two lines of fire had met and died quietly away for lack of fuel. The feeble flames that had resisted the draught and had crept onward over the long stretch of dry grass were easily brushed out by the boys and Mr. Lee.

When that was accomplished, the danger was chiefly over; still there remained scattered over the blackened region burning trees up which the flames were swirling to the very limbs; and these at any moment might fall, or throw a burning branch into the unburned district, and thus start a new fire.

Mr. Lee took all possible precautions against such an unfortunate occurrence, sweeping down the flames from such trees as it was possible to save, and burning the grass away in wide circles about burning trees that stood dangerously near the limits of the unburnt region.

The boys darted briskly about, lending a helping hand here, using their pine-tops wherever there was need, shouting excitedly to one another, and enjoying not a little the novelty and fun. They looked like imps of darkness as they sprang about over the strangely charred and smoking ground, weirdly lighted and shadowed by the flaring light from the burning trees.

It was long past midnight when they turned their faces toward home, — such smutted, hollow-eyed faces! Nip was the only one whose complexion did not suffer from such begriming work.

But, oh, how tired they were! They did not realize it until they were washed; and then, when they tumbled into bed, every

bone in their bodies seemed to have the tooth-
ache. And their eyes were so heavy! They
would have time to think about the tramp
in the morning.

The morning, however, was well advanced
before they awoke from their sleep of ex-
haustion; and when they staggered stiffly
from the Owlets' Roost, they found that
their father had already harnessed Pacer
in the long wagon, and was about to start
with their prisoner to Grandma's Bay. He
questioned the boys closely about their
encounter with the tramp on the previous
night, and put the wig and beard into the
wagon.

"Had n't you better take Brer, or both
the boys with you?" Mrs. Lee asked.

"Oh, no; the boys had better stay here.
They 'd be apt to get a glimpse of the world
that they are better off without at present.
This man is an escaped convict, I am sure.
You need n't worry about me, Lyla. I shall

take old Snap and my rifle along; and if the fellow shows a disposition to resist, he 'll find that neither the dog nor I can be trifled with. He shall drive, and I shall sit behind. There 's not the least risk."

The boys did not know whether to be pleased or not at this summary disposition of their captive. They hated the sight of him, and yet they felt a sort of ownership in him, and rather wished that they might have a hand in delivering him over to the authorities. However, they never disputed their father's judgment; and they hurried about, helping to arrange for his departure.

It was when he was seated in the wagon in which he himself was obliged to drive to his own fearful destiny that the tramp faced about, and wrathfully shaking his fist at the boys, cried huskily, —

"You youngsters ain't a-goin' to forget me, — the man that you sent back to jail without his ever havin' done you a bit of harm! I ain't a-goin' to forget you, you bet! When I come to the gallows, I 'll think of those skulkin' youngsters that sent me there. I 'll curse — "

" Stop that, and drive on ! " thundered Mr. Lee ; and with the pressure of cold steel against his temple, the man obeyed.

The boys looked uneasily at each other, standing still where the wagon had left them.

" If he *did n't* hurt us, he would uv if he could uv. What else was he planning when he swore there at the fire and shook his fist toward the Water-Oaks ? " cried Gene, defensively.

" I don't see how we could have done anything else, especially when he took the rifle," said Brer, his face much troubled.

" He boun' kill somebody wiv Brer's rifle, suah, ef we-uns doan mek 'im drap it," was Nip's conviction.

" You did just right and bravely, boys," said Mamma, reassuringly. " The man is desperate and wicked, not fit to be at large, — a danger in any community. You need n't feel in the least troubled by his words. Don't think of them."

But the boys did think of them, — Brer and Gene, at least, — though they tried their best to forget them. They were not greatly troubled, of course, since Mamma had said they had done right; still it was not pleasant to think that they had sent a man to the gallows. Fortunately, they never knew positively that he was hung, though Mr. Lee, when he delivered him to the proper authorities, found out that he had been convicted of a very terrible crime. What the crime was, he never told the boys.

There was one agreeable circumstance connected with the adventure of the tramp that went far toward easing the boys' consciences. The judge had been so pleased with the story of their bravery in capturing the man that he had declared they ought to have at least the amount offered for capturing an incendiary, and since they had seen the man in the very act of firing the woods, they were fully entitled to the reward. So, upon his return, their father smilingly gave to both Brer and Gene a gold-piece equal in value to a barrel of pecan-nuts in the fall.

CHAPTER VI.

BRER'S RIDE.

SPRING is such a rushing time under the water-oaks that the boys had at this season but little time for sport; but they had such jolly rollicking times over their work that they enjoyed it almost as much as play. Moreover, it was such a pleasure to them to feel that they were helping, and to hear their father say:—

"I 'm right proud of my boys. They can do almost as much work in a day as two full-grown men. They 're worth a dozen lazy no 'count niggers."

Nip, in a way, worked with the boys, of course; but somehow it was so unnatural for Nip to do anything but frolic, that it seemed almost as ridiculous to require work of him as of Flo or any of the other dogs.

Still, in spring every hand was needed; for besides the ordinary work, there was the ploughing and planting, cattle-hunting and branding, milking and churning, sheep-driving and sheep-shearing, fruit gathering and preserving, and a thousand and one other things to be done before the children could hope to see the sparkling waters of Grandma's Bay.

The first thing to be done was to feed up Muley-Mule a little with oats, so that she would have strength to plough the patches. Mr. Lee often suffered greatly from hoarseness in those days, for Muley-Mule was so stubborn and so weak, and the "po' pine lan'" so clayey and rough, that a tremendous amount of *geeing* and *hawing* was necessary before all the patches were furrowed. But the ploughing, sooner or later, was always accomplished, and Muley-Mule was turned forth again to enjoy her life of undisturbed leisure. The poor creature really did enjoy life at this season. It was the happiest time of the year for her. It is true, the measure of oats was no longer doled out to her; but that was of no consequence when tender sweet grass was springing up all through the burnt regions, making beautiful green slopes for the long shadows of the pines to stretch across, and, what Muley-Mule cared for, affording delicious pasturage upon which she could feast her ribs full, with a delightful sense of deserving from work well done.

The old mule actually became fat and frisky from good living. At night she would come trotting gayly back to the trough with her ears coquettishly cocked, and her nose comically smutted from contact with the fire-blackened ground.

Brer, always busy filling the trough at the time of Muley-Mule's visit, would greet her comical appearance with a derisive shout, while Nip, usually Brer's shadow, would address her tauntingly, —

"Heah come de Beauty ob de piney woods to look at herself in dis yer fine lookin'-glass. Hi, dar, Muley-Mule! yo' done forgit wash yo' face an' comb yo' ha'r, an' put de powda on. Doan go fo' to put yo' triflin' nigga face in dis yer fine basin w'at quality ho'ses gwine drink from."

Muley-Mule, being so comfortable in body, was too amiable in mind to resent this impudence, except by a provoking turn of her long left ear, and perhaps by a longer draught of water than necessary, thereby forcing Brer to draw an extra bucketful from the well. And every bucket counted; 8,395 a year was Brer's reckoning, averaging twenty-three per day,—sometimes more, sometimes fewer, usually more.

There were the two buckets on the back gallery to be kept full of the sweet sparkling water from the new well, also Aunt Nance's buckets in the kitchen. As the new well was furnished with a nice new pump, drawing the house water was a comparatively light task; but it seemed to Brer that the two buckets in the old well must be constantly coming up and going down, in order to keep the trough from going dry. It must be confessed that he sometimes grumbled over the lavish use of water under the water-oaks; but as he really took great pride in keeping buckets and trough sparkling to the brim, it is possible that this grumbling was indulged in for the sake of rousing Gene to controversy rather than to express any discontent with his work.

It was Gene's nominal duty to chop the light wood that his father hauled with old Pacer from the woods. In summer of course this task was trifling; but in winter, especially during a cold snap, when the people under the water-oaks had no idea of stinting themselves in the use of wood, or of keeping doors closed, it was by no means light work to keep Aunt Nance's wood-box full, and the piles of back-logs and light wood in the gallery up to a respectable height. At these times Mr. Lee and Brer always came to his assistance; but the responsibility of the job was Gene's, and the whacking of his fine sharp axe or the trundling of his new wheel-barrow might be heard at any moment. But he had his reward, not only in the consciousness of well-doing, but in his supreme satisfaction at night when the back-logs were laid and the light wood skilfully adjusted, and he lay on the hearth-rug watching the red flames smile and roar up the chimney, and felt that he had furnished the fuel for such luxurious warmth and glorious light.

When Brer, with a great show of being imposed upon, would count up his water-buckets, Gene would cry scornfully, "Draw-

ing water, — that's nothing! Cutting light-
ud now, — that takes muscle! It takes a
man to swing an axe and haul wood! How
many stick do you reckon I cut in a year?
You could n't count 'em!"

"I could count them in two minutes.
Just try watering this family one day, and
you 'll see who does the work. If I was n't
ashamed to do such baby work, I 'd change,"
Brer would remark with provoking condescension.

"Oh, yes, change! You 're too sharp to
change. Come on, let 's."

"Black-jack 's betta 'n white oak!"

This sharp interruption, if the boys were on
the gallery steps, would sound from the ridge-
pole directly over their heads; if they were
at the light-wood pile, it would drop from the
cedar branches above, repeated immediately
on this side of the roof, in an instant on the
other, in the tree under which they stood;

from the far edge of the grove, or after an instant's pause, from the distant patches.

"Black-jack's betta 'n white oak!"

With a whoop, the boys would start in pursuit, for of course it was Nip mimicking the whippoorwill that haunted the clearing in the moonlight nights of summer, hiding herself in the dark branches, and persisted in shouting out for half the night, in rapid, shrill, and positive iterations, the trite opinion that black-jack is better than white oak, as if any one would take the trouble to notice her, except with a pine-knot, if one could only get good aim.

It was far easier to make a good shot at Nip than at the sly night bird, cunning and spry though the little darky was; but it was only with harmless pine-burrs that the boys would pelt him until he would drop upon them, and all three boys, urged on by the wild barking of the dogs and the excited cries of the girls, would have a glorious tumble that would effectually banish any remaining feelings of rivalry between the drawer of water and the hewer of wood.

The other daily chores of the boys were light, — corn-husking for the horses, corn-shelling for Mamma's turkeys and chickens, feeding the few cattle that were kept about the place the year around for the scant supply of milk that could be drawn from their shrivelled bags, penning and unpenning the yearlings, feeding the shotes. Working together and with Nip made these duties fun pure and simple, unless, indeed, they happened to interfere with the more urgent occupation of trailing a rabbit, treeing a squirrel, or shooting doves and partridges in the pasture.

Sometimes Neal and Joy, for the proud privilege of enjoying the boys' society, would make a pretence of helping with the husking or the shelling, but the little girls were usually content to devote the moments that

they could snatch from play to helping
Mamma feed the turkeys and chickens, to
hunting hidden nests, and to nursing motherless, downy pee-wees and wee-wees.

In the planting season, in order to leave
Gene at liberty to help his mother garden,
old Pete was summoned to help Mr. Lee and
Brer seed the patches. Pete was a shiftless
worker, a very unequal substitute for Gene.
He was a charmingly social old darky, however; and the boys immensely enjoyed having him about. He was wonderfully weather-
wise and Bible-wise. The boys delighted in
asking him questions to draw out profoundly
ridiculous answers. His self-confidence was
never in the least shaken by the failure of
the weather to come up to his prophecies;
and although he had forfeited his member-
ship to more than one church from his utter
inability to "tell de truf," still he emphatically assured the boys that he "knowed his
Bible," and to prove his religious tendencies

lifted up his voice over his hoeing and rolled forth original psalm-tunes in such prodigious volume that the clearing fairly rang with hallelujahs.

Labor was not congenial to Pete. When Mr. Lee and Brer were absent, he usually sat in the shade of the fence and snoozed; or if he were lonely, he would try to entice the boys out for company by loud and importunate cries for "wata."

"Oh, yes, I reckon Pete thinks we 're his niggers," Gene would remark sarcastically, giggling at the notion; but finally, when he had sufficiently enjoyed Pete's calls, he would fill the tin bucket and with Nip trot out to the patch.

In the vegetable garden, Gene and his mother were head-gardeners, while Nance and the girls assisted or bothered, as the case might be. Gene considered it a great privilege to be allowed to work here instead of in the patches, not only because he delighted to

work with his mother, whom he served with
beautiful devotion and gallantry, but also
because the entire process of gardening was
in itself such a pleasure, — enriching and
cultivating the clayey soil into mellow, inviting beds, marking the straight grooves for
the seeds, dropping them in at nice depths
and covering them with careful patting.
After this came a little pause, when he
waited with suppressed excitement for the
magic work of the warm sun and the gentle
rains, until his keen eyes spied the first green
tips peeping forth in the identical places
where he had hidden the seeds away; then
followed the prolonged delight of watching
the little sprouts develop into lettuce, peas,
beans, Irish potatoes, tomatoes, cabbages,
squashes, just as he had planned; the blossoming, the forming, and maturing, and
finally the proud triumph of gathering the
messes for Aunt Nance to serve in savory
dishes to the admiring family.   Were ever

peas and beans and potatoes so delicious as Mamma's and his, or lettuce so crisp?

The next year, when Miss Sue, — the teacher from the North, — with the little Yankee, Tommy, was ruling the Owlets' Roost, she one day announced in the easy, offhand way she had of setting tasks that caused the school to lift its six hands in dismay, that each pupil should write, within a limited time, a composition on a subject of his own choosing.

After a soul-racking time of indecision, during which he suspended his pencil over every conceivable subject without being able to make a scratch, on the very last evening of grace, poor Gene sat down and wrote about his garden, and before he was half through telling about it, he had discovered to his astonishment that composition was great fun, after all; and not being able to write all he knew about gardening in one composition, he continued it the very next time that Miss Sue gave him an opportunity.

During the milking season, which began with the penning of the cattle in the spring, and lasted through summer-time, Gene had a task that was not nearly so much to his liking as gardening.

"Churning! I hate churning!" he even went so far as to declare. But that was either before or after the churning season; when he actually was at it he made no complaint. Indeed, from appearances, one might judge that he really liked it; at least, he made the most of it.

He was acknowledged the champion churner under the water-oaks, with the exception of his father.

"I reckon nobody carn't squeeze de milk so dry lak yo' pa. I 'low de shotes boun' miss de butta when yo' pa done churn de milk," was Nip's remark.

"I reckon Nip is right," Mr. Lee laughed, when he overheard it.

The churning was done immediately after breakfast, in the cool of the morning.

"Ready, Mamma!" Gene would call; and Mamma, with the sun-sweetened skimmer in her hand, would come down the gallery steps in her leisurely, smiling way, and cross the yard to the dairy under the shed of the new well.

When the yellow cream was skimmed from the pans, and the churn was filled and in position on a new yellow pine board, Gene, with the proud air of being monarch of all he surveyed, would take his seat of honor upon the wooden bench; pressing his little knees against the churn in as close imitation of Papa as possible, or with Nip's small legs clasped firmly about the base to steady it, he would begin the splash, splash, dash, splash.

Truly a more comfortable or charming spot for working on a warm spring morning it is impossible to imagine.

Throughout the clearing, over the patches, the air was glaring and hot, and quivering with the rays of the fierce Southern sun; but upon the house and the yard lay the dense, grateful shade of the water-oaks and the nut-trees, while a cool breeze from the distant bay swept softly under the branches, playing lightly with Mamma's hair, as she sat rocking gently on the corner of the gallery, with some sewing in her hands.

Under the deepest shade of the largest oak stood the dairy under the well-house, and before it sat Gene, splash-dash-splashing, and casting a stern and observant eye over the premises. For as churning is not an all-absorbing occupation, during this hour when his position as chief churner and only man about invested him with supreme authority,—Papa and Brer being out in the patches, or in the barn, or off cattle-hunting in the pines, — Gene devoted his chief energies to regulating affairs under the water-oaks, trying to discipline the inhabitants of the yard into something like orderly behavior.

The dogs he could manage easily. "Dogs had some sense." When he ordered them off, they went; and they knew enough not to worry the tantalizing cats in the kitchen door, when he was about.

Chickens, Susanna in particular, were everlasting torments, and refused to be anything else. Gene had his sling in his pocket and a pile of "rocks" at hand, with which to protect Mamma's plants on the gallery from their scratching; or if the chickens became indifferent to his shots, he ordered the girls to shoo them off. But the girls! They were the trial of the hour. The endeavor to make them behave was a task that never ended. During this hour that Gene gave to butter-making and to making them mind, the girls' mischief was as irrepressible as the steam in the molasses evaporator when a brisk fire crackled beneath it. Gene had no patience with them.

Two little black orphan pigs were being raised in the yard, who in their grunting fondness for buttermilk constantly threatened to overturn the churn, refusing to be quelled by the vigorous kicking of Gene's bare toes. As a two-edged punishment, struck at once against the girls and against the pigs, Gene commanded Nip to shut up the squealing little creatures in the girls' playhouse.

This was an insult to the girls, but such a ridiculous one that they could not help giggling as they peeked through the cracks at the unwilling tenants of their playhouse.

"Well," said Neal, at last, determined to make some condition on being forced to submit to this indignity. "If you want us to leave the pigs in there, you're bound to guess this riddle."

"Well, what is it?" demanded Gene, churning away indifferently.

"Now, Joy, don't you tell!" began Neal, her eyes wide and mysterious. "Now, let me see — "

"Mind you get it straight," interrupted Gene.

"Oh, hush! You mix me up. Oh, yes! 'What makes more noise than *one* pig under a gate?'"

"A hundred," answered Gene, promptly. "Run these puppies off, can't you?"

There were always a half-dozen or more of these short-legged, curious-eyed pups tumbling about the yard and drifting toward the churn; and tossing them off on his bare feet was much like rolling peas uphill.

The turkeys, kept in the yard until late in the day, lest they should hide their nests in the woods, were no trouble at all; they were only amusing, as they manœuvred in stately circles, or halted in gobbling chorus. Sometimes a strategic movement would result in the discovery of a snake, around which they

would draw their lines in closer and closer
circles, tiptoeing with the greatest caution,
cocking upon the squirming enemy first one
eye, then the other, and questioning one another with the liveliest concern with regard
to its probable nature. "Look out! See it?
See it! Peek! Peek? Pcek! Peek!"

This cry of course would summon Gene
from the churn, which he would surrender
to the girls with stern charges not to whip
the butter back nor to upset the churn, while
he marched manfully off to despatch the in-
truding reptile and relieve the anxiety of
the turkeys.

On the whole, the churning hour was
rather interesting to all concerned, especially
at the close, when buttermilk was served.

Indeed, compared with Brer's work, churning was mere sport. Gene never would have
felt the least twinge of the envy that sometimes caused him to watch with longing eyes
Brer's departure with his father, had he

known what it was to " rope calves " or to " cow-hunt."

To be sure, Brer had ample compensation for his harder work in his added sense of dignity from association with his father and the other men. Still, it was right hard for a little fellow — Mr. Lee himself acknowledged that — to tumble out of bed at the first pale glimmer of dawn, and go out through the warm moist air to the steaming cow-pen, to rope the hungry calves while Papa took his share of milk from the shrivelled bags of the poor piney-woods cows; but Brer did this every morning after the cows began to come up. At first he used to become dizzy from faintness; but his father would catch him up and lay him upon a board that was placed for the purpose across the corner of the rail fence, and leave him to come to himself while he went on to finish the milking before " sun-up."

In addition to his work in the pen, this

year, for the first time, Brer rode with the cow-drivers through the woods.

Mr. Lee was a good herdsman and a good shepherd. He knew at a glance every one of his cattle that ranged through the piney woods; and he remembered the face of every woolly back, though the sheep — aside from the one flock that slept under the cedar-grove — never approached the clearing except once a year, when they were gathered from far and near for the shearing.

Brer, however, and the other children — except, of course, Nip — could not tell their papa's cattle from those of Cousin Will or Uncle Jim, except for the brand; and to them the sheep looked as much alike as so many cotton-bolls.

It was Mr. Lee's wish that Brer should become more familiar with the herds and flocks. "So if anything should happen to me, my son, you would know how to manage for your mother and sisters," he said.

Accordingly, while still in knee-breeches, Brer mounted old Nag and rode off with the men.

Unlike bear-hunting and deer-hunting, cow-hunting is no sport. It is downright hard work, calling for great endurance of hunger and fatigue, and for much patience in driving stubborn cattle.

At an appointed time, the hunters — Uncle Jim, Cousin Will, and the other piney-woodsmen — meet at the Water-Oaks, or at some other homestead clearing, and separating in companies of twos and threes, scour the woods in all directions.

At night, each company drive such cattle as they have found, without regard to brands, into the pen of the most convenient clearing, often the hunters themselves remaining at the homestead of that clearing over night, to spare themselves and horses unnecessary travel. The next morning they go forth again, sometimes for a half-dozen successive mornings, until all the cattle are penned. Then, in turn, all the pens are visited, each driver claiming and branding his own cattle, and if he so chooses, separating them from the others to drive to his own cowpen. By the time that this is all accomplished, the hunters are pretty thoroughly exhausted.

"I don't know how the rest of you feel about it, but for my part I'm right glad I'm bound for home to-morrow, instead of for the woods," exclaimed Uncle Jim, on the last evening of the hunt.

He and Cousin Will were sitting with the family at the tea-table on the cool gallery, helping themselves to the bountiful supply of bacon and hominy, corn-pone and molasses.

"It's been a right jolly hunt for me, sure," said Cousin Will, reaching for the molasses-pitcher. "I'm mighty lucky this year. I've lost only two critters, and I've a right smart lot of young calves."

"It's been a lucky winter all round the piney-woods for cattle," remarked Mr. Lee. "I've only missed one cow-beast, and I'm sure I sighted her not two weeks ago, at the head of Bay River, too. Unless she's stuck in the swamp, she must be alive somewhere, with all this new grass to eat. I've a notion to make another day of it with Brer, and hunt her up."

"You'd best, if it's that pied cow you were telling of; she's worth the time. And I'd trust you, Bud, if you found nothing but a bag of bones, to put life into them." Cousin Will pushed back his chair, with a teasing laugh.

"Yes, Bud has sense enough to keep what he's got," said Uncle Jim. "He isn't going to leave half the butter in the milk for the hogs, either."

"You're right there, boys; I prefer to keep the butter for nearer kin," retorted Mr. Lee, with a good-natured twinkle in his eye. "If I do squeeze the milk for the butter, there are those who like to eat the butter, and they are right welcome to it," he added, not in the least offended by their teasing reference to his well-known habits of close economy and thrift.

"I'm mighty glad you feel that way, Bud," called Cousin Will, strolling to the other end of the gallery to light his pipe; "for I'm bound to drop in every time the wind blows toward the Water-Oaks. A cup of Lyla's coffee and a filling of her potato-pone are necessary once a month to keep me going."

"If you say so, Bud, I'll stay over and help hunt that cow," said Uncle Jim, as he rose and drew his tobacco-pouch from his pocket.

"Oh, no; just as much obliged, but Brer and I can manage first-rate, I reckon."

Early the next morning Uncle Jim and Cousin Will started for their homes on the

Bay, driving before them such cattle as they chose to milk during the summer.

Mr. Lee and Brer rode off too, but in an opposite direction. They turned their horses' heads toward the source of Bay River, and rode at a comfortable pace along the bridle-path.

The distance before them was long to the spot where Mr. Lee had last seen the pied cow; but they had the whole day for the hunt, and Jinny and Nag, having been jogging steadily all the week, were disposed to take their own time.

Toward noon, thunder-heads lifted above the pines in the far northwest, and the low mutterings of a storm sounded in the distance; but the clouds having threatened in this way every day of the past week, and then drifted around the hunters to empty their contents on some distant portion of the piney woods, Mr. Lee and Brer rode on in careless unconcern of the weather-signs.

They were as silent as two Indians, as they rode over the rounded knolls and sunny hollows of the open piney woods, across rough bowlder-strewed ledges, along the densely wooded course of winding branches, or paused a moment in the rippling fords while Jinny and Nag thrust their noses into the clear water. With no sound to disturb the ceaseless swishing of the pines overhead, save the steady trot, trot, trot, of their horses, the occasional sweet call of the meadow-lark in the sunny distance, and once the chopping of a woodman's axe, they passed through the long distances of the woods, over Gum-Tree Branch, across the resin-coated ground of the deserted turpentine still, past the deserted Holly place, with its open doors and fallen fences, near a cluster of silent negro cabins with the tall, lone chimney beyond them, marking the abandoned hearthstone of an old house.

Brer and Nag, following, jogged indifferently along. Jinny, however, leading the way, was wide awake, picking careful steps along the rain-washed trail, or over or around a fallen tree that blocked the path; while Mr. Lee, erect and intent, with keen eye, glanced sharply on every side for traces of the pied cow, or for tracks of " varmint," — enemies to his flocks and herds.

"Ah!" he exclaimed at last, bringing Jinny to an abrupt standstill. "Look yonder!" He pointed upward; and Brer, following his finger, after a moment of intent gazing, perceived a black speck up in the sky that, as he watched, grew gradually larger, descending into plain sight, at last, as a large long-winged buzzard.

" Look yonder!" he cried again, as more soaring specks appeared, seemingly from out the blue, and slowly dropped into view.

" They 're making for the swamp, sure. We 're too late to find the pied cow. It looks like the fire had driven her into the swamp, and the poor critter had n't strength to pull herself out. Go 'long, Jinny." As they rode forward, the region about the head of the river showed, by its blackened surface just beginning to brighten with the green tips of piercing grass-blades, that the woods here had just burned.

Having approached the thicket of the spring, Mr. Lee threw himself from Jinny, and handing the bridle to Brer, carefully examined the soft mud of the various paths that led under the thick underbrush of the swamp. He disappeared from view; but Brer could hear the breaking of twigs and swinging of branches as his father pushed his way through the dense, tangled bushes. He also could hear a significant sound that he knew well, — the slow flapping of the clumsy buzzards as they settled about the tempting feast that had drawn them down from the sky.

He was tired of the saddle, and thirsty, so

he dismounted ; and having tied the horses to a couple of gum-trees, he went down the path to the spring, where the water was always cool and sweet, under the white-stemmed magnolia-tree that shaded it and furnished a liberal supply of thick, shiny leaves for drinking-cups. He lingered a few moments in the delicious coolness, carelessly cutting his mark in the soft bark of the tree, while he vaguely wondered at the intense gloom of the place that the shade of the trees seemed hardly sufficient to cause.

Presently his father called him.

"Son ! Son !"

"Ho !" answered Brer, promptly.

Running back to the horses, he found his father already mounted on Jinny, and with Nag's bridle in his hand.

"Look sharp !" said Mr. Lee, who was anxiously scanning the sky. " The cow is swamped, and the buzzards have got her, and we 're in for a good wetting. We 'll make for old man Johnson's clearing. Keep Nag up right close, now."

Brer sprang to Nag's back, and the old horse instantly wheeled about and galloped rapidly after Jinny, who, under Mr. Lee's careful guidance, wound nimbly among the pines, springing lightly over fallen logs and avoiding sink-holes in a way astonishing, had not her rider been almost as familiar with every foot of piney-woods ground as with his own particular clearing under the water-oaks.

But the swift-coming storm was already upon them. The pine-tops were swaying and moaning restlessly in the rising wind; dense clouds were pressing heavily down, filling the woods with a gloom that was all a-quiver with lightning-flashes; the rolling of thunder broke into startling crashes, and large rain-drops were already falling.

"Look sharp!" shouted Mr. Lee over his shoulder, urging Jinny to greater speed, for he well knew the dangers from falling trees in a storm.

The storm rapidly increased in fury; great trees swayed threateningly; the rain swept down in sheets, soaking to the skin, and blinding both horses and riders. It was impossible to make headway in such confusion.

Mr. Lee suddenly turned Jinny into a sapling thicket and brought her to a standstill under the partial shelter of the young trees. Nag carried Brer close alongside. Then they waited, facing the storm, with their hats pulled over their eyes and their shoulders drawn shrinkingly up, for the tempest to spend its fury. The uproar was terrific. The thunder rolled and rattled and crashed; one dazzling flash of lightning instantly followed another; the rain beat upon them pitilessly, swirled and dashed against them from every direction by the wind-tossed saplings.

Shrinking from the flooding, smothering rain, Brer wondered why his father had not sought shelter behind some huge pine; but, as he grumbled to himself, came the prompt and emphatic answer, as if he had spoken. A sharp tearing and crackling sounded close at hand, followed by a loud, stunning thud that shook the very ground, and caused both horses to spring in terror. Brer almost fell from his saddle, but he recovered himself, and managed to keep hold of the bridle. Nag at once stood still, though Brer could feel her trembling under him. It was a falling tree. Brer had heard the sound many times, but always from a distance.

"A mighty close call," shouted Mr. Lee, bringing Jinny back to Nag's side, "but we 're one tree safer."

"Lightning struck?" yelled Brer.

"No, a rotten — Lor !"

There was a dazzling flash ; a frightful,

tearing crash. It seemed to Brer as if the very heavens were shattering and falling upon them. He instinctively fell forward upon Nag's neck; none too soon, for with a snort and a bound of terror, the old horse seized the bit, and dashed madly into the forest and the raging storm. Clinging desperately about her neck, and pressing closely with his body, Brer closed his eyes and held his breath in dreadful expectation that the next instant he would be dashed against a pine-tree or crushed beneath Nag in a sink-hole. But on and on and on they dashed, up and down, and through splashing water. Brer could not think, he could not even care, where Nag was taking him. He felt as if he were being whirled through a horrible, maddening dream — and suddenly came the end, as startling as the fall from a nightmare into a bed of down.

In a sickening second he felt himself torn from the saddle; but when he instinctively nerved himself for a shock, nothing followed.

Surely this was a dream. He felt about timidly at first, then he struck out wildly in vain attempts to grasp something with hands or feet, but, strangely, there was nothing.

"Doan flounder 'roun' so lak a turtle," remonstrated a gasping voice above him.

Brer opened his eyes, expecting to see Nip astride the footboard. But no, he was not in bed; he was somewhere out in the piney woods. He was suspended in some way, face downward. All he could see was a narrow water-filled trail, running through the pine-straw a few feet below.

"Watch out whar yo' gwine strike; I 's boun' drap yo'," said the breathless voice again.

Brer chose the dryest-looking spot beneath him, and came down lightly on his hands and bare feet. He was up like a spring;

and looking above, he spied Nip's lithe figure pulling itself up on a leafy branch.

"Is that you, Nip?" he asked, still stunned by his tempestuous ride, and hardly venturing to believe his senses.

"I reckon dis nigger am Nip," replied the voice.

"What you doing up there in this wet?"

"I's a-comin' down, Brer."

The rain had stopped as suddenly as it had begun. The clouds were blown over, and the wind that drove them was gone. The sun had burst forth warmly upon the fresh, dripping woods.

Nip came down with a shower of drops.

"Does yo' reckon Nag's done kilt herself, Brer?" he asked.

"I don't know. Where is she? Come on; we'll follow her up. Where are we, anyway?"

Brer was thoroughly bewildered.

"Yer we is, under de 'simmon-tree."

Brer gazed about in amazement. Sure enough, here he was on the very edge of the water-oak clearing. Nag had come straight for home by the trail they had travelled in the morning.

"Oh, Nag's safe and sound in the barn, I reckon," he exclaimed in relief.

"I reckon ole Nag's so scart she doan see de washout in de gully, case I done hear her yell lak she done fall right in."

"The trail washed into the gully! Then she's bound to be down."

They ran along the wet trail to the head of the gully. The broad overhanging edge across which the trail ran had broken off abruptly, and carried to the depths below the cluster of saplings that had grown upon it.

Poor Nag, alas! had been too frenzied to notice the break in the trail, for there she lay, quite on the other side of the gully bottom.

" She was going so fast she just flew right across, and came whack ! head-first, against that far side," cried Brer.

" I reckon ole Nag done broke her-all neck," said Nip, as they made their way down through the wet sand.

He was right. The horse's head was bent sideways right under the body, and she was quite dead.

" What 'll Papa say ? " lamented Brer.

" I reckon he 's boun' feel right bad 'bout ole Nag," said Nip, ruefully.

" I hope *he 's* all right." Brer looked anxiously up to the edge of the gully. " Come on ! I never thought; Jinny 's bound to do just like old Nag."

" Miss Lee doan ride wiv his eyes shut," said Nip, reassuringly, as they climbed hurriedly up.

" But he might be on the watch-out for me — There he is ! Pa*pa !* Here; all right ! "

Mr. Lee had checked Jinny on the very edge of the gully, whence he was gazing down at Nag's body with a horror-stricken face.

At Brer's call, he answered with a hoarse cry of relief, and then he slowly dismounted as if he had been bound by some dreadful spell.

"Thank God!" he exclaimed devoutly, when Brer appeared over the edge of the gully. "I thought sure you were lying under Nag down yonder. How did you escape?"

"Why, I—I do' know. Nip grabbed me."

"Nip grabbed you! How in this world could he do that?"

"I do' know. The first thing I knew, Nag was gone, and I was swinging in air. Then in a minute Nip let go, and I came down to ground."

"But where was Nip?"

"He was in the persimmon-tree, and when Nag came a-tearing along the trail

under that long branch, he just — I say,
Nip, how 'd you manage to keep a grip on
the tree ?"

" I dunno, Brer. I jes' twis' my legs
roun' lak I does in de water-oaks."

" Did n't it almost yank you in pieces to
pull him off ?" asked Mr. Lee.

" 'Peard lak Brer ain't gwine let ole Nag
go, an' I 'lowed I 's gwine 'long wiv Nag
an' Brer into de gully an' leave my legs
behind ; but Brer, he done 'cide to 'bide wiv
me, so I doan dis'point Neal an' tote her de
dewberries w'at I promis' her."

" So you were out after dewberries, were
you, when the rain came on ? That 's how
you happened to see the washout."

" Yas, sah."

" How 'd you happen to be up in the
persimmon-tree ?"

" I 'lowed de fiah ain't gwine run down
from de sky on a 'simmon-tree, de pine-trees
a-reachin' up so high fo' it."

"And when you saw old Nag a-thundering along, you just swung under and caught onto me!"

"It's right lucky for you — for all of us — that Nip happened to be up there and had the grip to hold you, else you'd be down there with poor Nag this minute." Mr. Lee spoke very soberly; but he roused himself in a moment. "Come, we must get that saddle and bridle off, and hurry home to your mother; she'll be worried about us."

The fact that Nip had saved Brer's life was fully appreciated by the people under the water-oaks, as they showed by special kindness to him; they were very grateful, but no one thought it necessary to say so, Nip himself least of all. He understood their feelings without the saying, just as Flo or Snap would have understood, and he was perfectly satisfied. Perhaps Neal expressed more appreciation of his deed

than any one else. She made him re-
late the occurrence over and over again:
where he had found the berries; how he
had run when it began to rain; just how
he had happened to go around by the gully;
and why he scrambled up into the persimmon-tree when he heard that awful clap of
thunder; what he had thought when he
heard Nag coming, and saw Brer, — everything; she even inquired anxiously if his
joints were not loose.

"Papa," she asked, after due considera-
tion, "don't you think we ought to give
Nip a collar, like Cousin Will did old dog
Bishop, when he pulled little Lollie out of
the creek?"

CHAPTER VII.

GENE OVERCOMES OLD BILLY.

"Ow!" cried Gene, shrinking as if he had been seized with hot pincers. "Just look a-here, what I've done, will you? It makes me sick!"

Brer had just released a sheep from the shearing-bench, and was watching with a grin the awkward, shorn, sheepish creature, embarrassed by its own lightness, bound uncertainly back to the flock, and huddle in, as if to hide its unbecoming nakedness.

At Gene's outcry, he crossed over to his bench.

"Gee! I should think it would make you sick! What's the use of cutting into a critter like that?"

"If the thing would squirm, and not lie there like a log, it would n't get cut into. How 's a fellow to know whether he 's cutting skin or wool ? I don't believe a sheep would budge if I cut its leg off ! " exclaimed Gene. " I 'd hate to be a sheep, without a spark of spirit ! "

" Suppose you catch a sheep, and let your brother finish shearing that one," said Mr. Lee, crossing from his own bench to examine Gene's work. " You have managed to cut that poor thing up pretty badly, I declare. Here, catch me that ewe yonder."

Gene made a dash that scattered the flock, and clutching the ewe by its wool, held it with a determined grip, though the frightened creature dragged him all about the pen in its efforts to escape.

" Come and get her, Papa," he cried, between his teeth. Then addressing the struggling sheep, he muttered, " No, you don't ! You just stay where you are."

"Hold on! Don't let her get away with you!" cried Mr. Lee, who with Brer was stopping work to enjoy the tussle. "Here you are, old sheep! You might as well give up first as last when Gene gets hold of you."

He lifted the sheep easily, stretched it on the bench, and deftly secured its crossed fore-legs under a nicely contrived strap, while Nip fastened the hind-legs in the same way.

Gene sat panting on an inverted nail-keg. "That ewe's mighty strong," he gasped, "but I was just bound to keep her."

The open centre of the new barn had been transformed into a sheep-pen. A shearing-bench had been built across one end, and a fence at the rear enclosed considerable space, confining the sheep convenient for catching. The barn was shady and comfortable, with a cooling current of air drawing constantly through it, making it a pleasant working-place even on a day too dazzling to be looked at and too warm for gathering peaches.

At times the entire family assembled here, even Mamma with the rest, a great apron over her dress, over-sleeves on her arms, shearing, shearing, shearing, the heavy fleeces from the panting, pink-skinned sheep.

Nip's place was on the shearing-bench, where it was his business to aid in strapping the captured sheep, keep track of the shears, and carry off the fleeces when they were taken from the uncomplaining sheep.

Neal and Joy were on the bench too, fidgeting about, and running slyly from one end to the other for something that they had forgotten, and that they must have on the instant. They were trying hard to keep still, —oh, yes, desperately hard, for the permission to stay up there was good only so long as they did not bother. If Brer and Gene had not been so fussy there would not have been the least trouble, but the boys always were picking at them, poor things! Papa and Mamma did not mind their fun, and

Mamma, when she was helping Gene shear, always let them pet the poor tied sheep, keeping so nice and still.

"You're such a fine sheep-catcher, suppose you catch one for me. I'm about through with this fellow," said Brer, who was clipping away with all his might, for it was his ambition to shear as many sheep a day as his father. Already he could shear as many as Cousin Will, for he was wonderfully skilful with the clippers; and each day he increased his number. Gene pounced upon a black ewe; and after the usual scurry about the pen, amid the excited screaming of Neal and Joy, he brought it triumphantly to Brer's bench.

"There's some fun in that," he exclaimed, drawing a long breath of satisfaction when he had helped Brer to lift and strap the sheep.

"I'd a heap rather chase them than clip, clip, clip, snip, snip, snip, cutting great streaks out of them, and they having no more sense than to let me.   Ugh! it makes my flesh creep."

"Suppose you do all the catching, then, and let those that know the difference between wool and mutton do the shearing," suggested Brer.

"All right, if you and Papa 'll give me a cent for every one I catch," agreed Gene.

"I 'll do it if Papa will. Shall we, Papa?" asked cautious Brer.

"Yes, it 's a bargain. Fetch me old Billy, Gene, while I finish this one."

Billy was an old merino ram who had once been a pet under the water-oaks, but at last he had wandered off with the flock. He soon had forgotten his old play-fellows, for when he had spent a year in the woods and came back at the shearing season, he refused to take the least notice of the children; and when they made friendly advances, he received them with a sullen lowering of his immense spiral horns.

Billy did not like the shearing any more than the other sheep, and he had been standing all the morning with his head thrust gloomily into a corner, casting angry sheep's-eyes whenever a raid was made upon the flock for another victim.

He always made fierce resistance when his turn came, and Mr. Lee had no idea that Gene would make an attempt to catch the ugly-tempered animal.

Gene, however, having made a bargain, had no idea of backing out of it the very first thing.

Billy was rather small, but he was very strong. It sometimes was as much as Mr. Lee himself could do to catch him and strap him down. The great thing was to get a proper hold of him, to begin with.

Gene carefully examined Billy's position; it seemed to him that it was very favorable. All that he need do was to steal slyly up, land on Billy's back with a quick spring, and pull in the sheep's fore-feet, so that he would be on his knees before he could move and bring those terrible horns into play.

Accordingly, Gene advanced as quietly as possible among the scattering flock, pretending to have his eye on an old Roman-nosed ewe that stood not far behind the ram, for he knew how watchful and keen Billy was. If he should have a suspicion that he was Gene's object, the chance would be lost.

Gene was very successful in getting quite near, and he had just spread himself for a short run and a spring, when the ram wheeled and darted forward. Before Gene could think, he was lying flat on the sheep's back with both hands buried in the thick wool, and with his feet closely wrapped about Billy's stout neck.

Now began a wild backward ride, that was like a dizzy tangle of circles to Gene. Around and around dashed Billy, scattering the astonished flock before him, tossing his head angrily, prancing stiffly on his four short legs, whirling dizzily in vain effort to throw his rider off, and at last, having successfully dodged Mr. Lee and Brer in their efforts to head him off and corner him, he made a reckless dash at the gate; and rising with a determined spring, he came stolidly down on the other side.

"Let him go!" shouted Mr. Lee.

But Gene did no such thing. He dug his hands more securely into the matted wool. "Let him go!" Not he, after being served such a trick! Billy might bolt over a pine-top for all he cared. He reckoned he could stand it if Billy could. No, sir, he had got Billy, and he meant to keep him.

Straight ahead into the piney woods Billy dashed, with quick, short bounds. Gene renewed his clutch and lifted his head to see what path they were leaving behind them. Ah! he saw. Billy was on his way back to the pasturing-grounds, where he never had been encumbered with such loads. But Billy's pasture was on the far side of Fish River, and Gene was by no means inclined to travel so far from the Water-Oaks. Cautiously he lowered his feet, and gradually worked up to a sitting posture. The sensation of riding backward was very queer, especially at Billy's rough gait. But to one who had had some experience with horses of various dispositions, and also with Muley-Mule, it was not impossible to keep one's seat, especially so near the ground.

But although he might stand the ride, Gene had no desire to go on. He could think of no possible way to stop the ram, but at least he could bother him a little.

Securing a firmer grip of the wool with one hand, he reached carefully around with the other until he could grasp one of Billy's horns, and pulled it backward.

Billy jerked his head angrily, but Gene held on, though the strain wrenched him severely.

The ram pranced fiercely at this fresh insult, but he was obliged to slacken his pace, and presently Gene noticed that instead of dashing madly ahead, his course was becoming more and more curved. He exerted himself to pull the head still farther aside, so that Billy, in following his nose, made a wide circuit, instead of moving so rapidly forward. The ram was losing both spirit and strength under the human burr that clung so persistently to his back, and suddenly both were pretty well knocked out of him by the blind force with which he ran against a pine-tree. As Billy came to an abrupt stop, and stood half stunned by the unexpected blow, the thought flashed through Gene's head that, after all, his trouble had only begun. Bringing Billy to a standstill was all very satisfactory, but how in the world could he ever make the stubborn creature go back to the Water-Oaks?

Fortunate things happen •in the piney

woods, however, as well as out in the world and in books. Just as Billy began to recover from the shock, and was showing very plainly, by a series of butts at the offending tree, that his ugly temper was by no means subdued, Gene heard the welcome music of old Pete's voice. The old darky was approaching along the trail from which Billy's twisted horn had led him astray. Old Pete was singing a psalm-tune at the top of his rich, bass voice, emphasizing it at the end of each stanza by a prolonged roar and an energetic lurch of the hoe which he carried. Although his own uproar prevented his hearing Gene's outcry, he quickly spied the queer steed and his rider; for they do say a piney-woods darky can see through the back of his head, his sight is so keen.

He ended his song with a wild whoop, and came hurrying forward.

"Law, Gene, what fo' yo' an' Billy 'way out yer, behaving lak yo' ain't got no sense?

What fo' doan yo' sit roun' fo'wa'ds an' tell yo' fool ho'se he carn't butt no trail t'rough a pine-tree? 'Pears lak ole Billy boun' jerk yo'-alls to pieces. Bes' git down from dat fine ho'se an' let him root up dat tree by hisself."

"I ain't going to get down. The old thing brought me here, and he's got to take me home. I say, Pete, I wish you would whack him with that hoe, and make him quit jarring so."

"All right, Gene. Jest look out fo' yo'-alls legs an' I'll hoe his wool fo' him. Whoa, you Billy-ho'se! What fo' yo' doin' Gene dat-a-way? I's gwine larn yo' some sense."

With this, Pete brought his hoe down with a resounding blow on the sheep's side, and dodged behind the pine-tree. But Billy saw him, and darted after him with a speed that caused old Pete to spin around and around before the threatening horns, and almost flung Gene off by centrifugal force.

"Make for home!" yelled Gene. "If

you 'll make him follow you home, I 'll make Papa give you a nickel's worth of tobacco," he gasped.

" All right, Gene ; old Pete ain't gwine lose dat tobac, suah."

He shook his hoe in the angry ram's face and darted away, Billy bounding after him. More than once the old darky was forced to pause and circle around a pine-tree, while he recovered breath ; and twice, when Billy came to a stubborn standstill, as if he half suspected the game, Pete was obliged to stir up his wrath with the hoe.

At last they reached the clearing, and after a moment's breathing spell behind the last pine, old Pete offered his last insult to Billy by tossing a pine-burr into his face, and flew straight toward the barn, Billy leaping after him in blind rage.

Mr. Lee had just saddled Jinny to give chase to the runaways, when he spied them coming at full tilt. He directed Brer to open the gate of the sheep-pen wide, while he himself stood in readiness to lay hands on Billy.

With a yell, old Pete rushed into the pen and bounded to the shearing-bench; and Billy, regardless of everything but his tormentor, was drawing himself up to follow, when Mr. Lee's ready hand seized him and brought him to his knees. In an instant Gene had slid down, and swept the hind-feet of the ram off the ground; and Billy, spite of his struggles, was soon securely strapped down upon the bench. He made two or three more efforts to escape, but finding them futile, he fell back and lay breathing heavily.

Gene sank upon the nail-keg and gave vent to his excitement in an hysterical burst of laughter and tears. They all roared and shouted with laughter, but not one shed a tear with him, except those that rose to their eyes from the distress of laughing.

"I reckon you won't be so keen to catch any more sheep," laughed Brer, holding his sides.

"Yes, *sir*," cried Gene, starting suddenly from his collapsed condition. "I'm going to catch every single one of them!"

And so he did.

CHAPTER VIII.

LITTLE LAND-LUBBERS ON GRANDMA'S BAY.

"OH, Mamma, *why* can't we take Nip to Grandma's Bay?" coaxed Joy, nestling in her mother's lap and twining her soft arms about her neck. "Just this once!"

"Do let him go, Mamma; Nip just ought to see that bay. He thinks it 's nothing but a pond. Why can't he go?" begged Gene.

"There is no spare room in the wagon, and Grandma expects only five of us," answered Mrs. Lee. Then, with a twinkle in her eye, she suggested, "If one of you should stay here with your father, to help him milk and churn, there would be room for Nip."

This was an exceedingly awkward proposal. The children flushed and ahemmed, but they said never a word for full two minutes. They carefully avoided looking at one another, their whole attention being suddenly concentrated upon the sweet and juicy water-melon of which each held a huge pink chunk. One not knowing that they had been indulging in the delights of water-melon for a week, or not having seen the huge pile that the boys had hauled in from the patch in the early morning and laid in the coolest corner of the dining-room, might have thought that they were so many little epicures enjoying the one melon of the season, such intense and critical devotion did they devote to their luscious handfuls.

The children were gathered about Mamma's chair, — Neal and Joy and Nip on the gallery floor, the two boys on the steps, all lying about in easy attitudes, with the comfortable air of having nothing to do. For at last the busy time was over, and the

well-earned, delightful rest had come, when
they could lounge all day on the gallery,
shaded from the blinding glare of the sun
by the thick canopy of the water-oaks, and
fanned by the cool, spicy breezes from Grandma's Bay.

They had helped Mamma prepare the fruit
for preserving, and at the same time they
had managed to stow away in their small
bodies an incredible quantity of honey-burst
figs, luscious peaches, and cool melons. Such
congenial occupation did not interfere in the
least with their chattering; all their plans
for Grandma's Bay were made, and to-morrow — why, they really were going!

The figs had been soured by the last rain ;
but there were still tempting peaches on the
trees and great round melons in the patch.
These they were willing to leave for Papa,
but Nip — they hated to leave Nip behind.

Which one of them could be generous
enough to give up that long-anticipated

visit in favor of Nip? Each waited to give the others a chance to make this praise-worthy sacrifice.

At last Neal asked rather doubtfully, but with a sly twinkle, very much like Mamma's, in her eye, —

"Would n't Grandma be *dreadfully* disappointed if she should see Nip a-sitting up behind Papa instead of — Brer?"

"I reckon Grandma will expect to see Brer," answered Mamma, with a smile.

"Or just Nip, instead of Gene, sitting on the trunk beside me?" continued Neal.

"Just Nip, instead of *you*, sitting on the trunk beside *me*, you mean," interrupted Gene. "Why, Grandma would send you all back if you left me behind. You 'd just better not try it."

"Grandma said *I* must come. She said she reckoned that when I came to the Bay, I 'd be as straight as Aunty," cried Neal, defiantly.

"You'd better not go, then, I can tell you, Miss. There you sit, bent up like a jack-knife!" exclaimed Brer.

Neal straightened up with a jerk, and sat as upright and stiff as if a cold iron rod had been run down her back.

"See here, Joy, seeing you're so anxious, *you* might stay at home. Nip would look right pretty, sitting up there in Mamma's lap. Grandma wouldn't miss such a mite as you," suggested Brer.

"Yes, she would," cried Joy; "wouldn't she, Mamma? I won't let Nip sit on Mamma's lap."

"What fo' yo'-alls w'ar yo'selves out?" here piped up Nip, who had been eating his juicy melon with unrestrained gusto, and listening to this squabble with an air of supreme unconcern. "Nip ain't gwine fool 'way his time holdin' on de aidge of Grammer's Bay, whar de suns an' de moons an' de stars goes a-slippin' down into de wata

an' git drownded; he gwine 'bide right yer
on dry lan' an' watch out fo' de grapes to
git ripe."

"He is the biggest goose about the Bay,
Mamma. He just ought to go next year,
anyway. Papa might get old Pete to stay
with him, if the dogs would n't eat him
up."

"Next year, I 's boun' cotch de ole ha'nt
moon an' mek him tote me down Grammer's
Bay," said Nip, looking up at the silver boat
just gliding from behind a cloud into the
rosy sunset sky.

"Then you can go a-rowing in it on the
Bay," cried Neal, forgetting her prim attitude, and bending her head quite to the
gallery floor to catch a better glimpse of
the new-moon skiff. "I 'm going to look
for you every single night."

"Perhaps you 'll see him this year," said
Mr. Lee, who had come from the orchard
with a hatful of peaches. and having seated

himself beside Mamma, was liberally tossing the pink balls to the children. " I 've been thinking of bringing Uncle Jim's Frank back into the piney woods to give him a chance to get over the fever. If he comes, I 'll just hand Nip here over to the man in the moon, and let him go along down to the Bay."

Joy clapped her hands gleefully.

" When Nip comes, we 'll just have heaps of fun," she cried, as if she had been doubtful of good times without him.

The next morning, by the light of the stars that seemed to have waited a little later than usual to see them off, the children shouted an excited farewell to their dusky playfellow, who, upside down on the gate-post, was waving them a parting salute with his little bare foot. " Mind you come as soon as Papa lets you off," was Brer's last command.

" All right, Brer. Yo'-alls jes' watch out

an' see me come a-sailin' down out ob de sky some fine night."

"I'm going to watch every night after I say my prayers," screamed Joy, bouncing in her mother's arms.

"Me too," echoed Neal, jogging along behind on the hard trunk, between Brer and Gene.

But by noon, when Pacer, panting and wet from his twenty-mile pull, drew them forth from the piney woods, and stopped at Grandma's gate, on the very brink of the blue sparkling bay, all thoughts of Nip had fled from their minds; nor did they once think of him again that day, and at night Neal and Joy were almost too tired to say their prayers, and the boys were too full of frolic to remember anything.

As for the days that followed, they were too full for thinking. To begin with, the children must explore Grandma's premises and the whole extensive playground of the

Bay shore, to see if everything was as they had left it. They examined with critical eye the scuppernong vine and the orange orchard to estimate how many bottles of wine Aunty would make this season, and how many bags of oranges would come to the Water-Oaks in the fall.

They sipped a healthful draught from Sulphur Spring, and rushed wildly to the cool, dark waters of Deep-Hole to wash the disagreeable mineral taste from their mouths. There were the twin elms to be visited, and their famous dam of the run in the dell.

After all their haunts had been duly inspected, they must conquer their shyness and make acquaintance with the city children who had come across the Bay for the summer. And then the days were so crowded with excitement and frolic, and the nights were so heavy with sleep, that there was no opportunity to think of Nip.

But one morning there was Nip sitting with
Flo on the steps of Grandma's front gal-
lery, gazing with soft, observant eyes on
Grandma's Bay.

"Why, you Nip!" shouted Brer, with
mingled joy and astonishment. The boys,
rushing from their room for their early
plunge in the bay, had almost stumbled
over the unexpected apparitions.

"Flo too!" yelled Gene, dancing about
on one foot in his delight. "See, she is n't
afraid of me down here!"

Neal and Joy came pattering out in their
night-gowns. Neal stared at Nip with great
round eyes.

"Oh, Nip, did you come in the moon, sure
enough?" she demanded.

"Where 's the moon-man?" queried Joy,
glancing around.

"Why, there 's the man and there 's his
dog," responded Brer, roguishly pointing to
Nip and Flo. "What are your eyes for,

I 'd like to know? If you 'd ask him where he has moored the moon, there 'd be some sense in it."

"Where did you, at Grandma's wharf?" innocently demanded Joy; but the next instant she was shouting with the boys over her own foolish question.

" De moon done git swamp in Grammer's Bay; I done see it go down," announced Nip, who was grinning and tumbling all about in his delight at being again with the children.

Neal and Joy were a trifle startled by this bold statement, but before they could question it, Brer ordered them in to dress, while he and Gene led Nip off for his first swimming-lesson.

Nip, however, needed no instruction in the art of swimming. The very first time that the boys pushed him from the wharf, with the severe but benevolent intention of compelling him to strike out, to swim or sink, he rose like a duck to the surface, and plunged and darted about as if he had been born and raised in the water instead of nobody knows where. Brer and Gene and all the other white boys were as clumsy as porpoises beside the swift, gliding little darky. They tried to learn how he darted about so easily, but Nip could not teach them.

" 'Pears lak I does jes' lak de swallows does up yonda in de sky," was all that he could tell them.

Grandma's Bay seems to have been made especially for children to play in, for a hard, sandy floor extends for almost half a mile straight out from the shore, perfectly level and smooth, so that one can wade in with perfect security, without the least fear of plunging over one's head into a deep hole. When the tide was out, Neal and Joy could run far out before the smooth water came up to their necks; but when the tide was in, they stayed under the bath-house;

and when the wind blew the water into rolling waves that take one's breath away, they did not go in at all.

But the boys did. When a storm was raging in the gulf, and the soft, south wind blew in strong, warm gusts over the bay, ploughing deep furrows in the water and tossing it up in foaming white-caps, the boys had the jolliest times of all. It was such fun to run before the swiftly chasing waves, to leap over them, one after another, as they rolled rapidly in to shore, or to dash under the white breakers, and come up, gasping and dripping, on the other side just in time to meet another.

But the greatest sport of all was one forbidden to Brer and Gene. Some of the boys who had lived on the bay all their lives, and were as much at home in the water as on the sandy shore, used to row out into the storm-tossed waves; and when they were quite beyond the wharves that run out from the villas along shore, they would unfurl a great sail. This the wind would catch instantly, and send the boat skimming like a bird through the dashing spray at a speed that took their breath away, and then, with a sudden, mischievous puff, it would dip the sail under the waves, and the boys would be floundering in the water or clinging to the edge of the boat. These boys would urge and tease Brer and Gene to join them, and when the two boys dutifully refused, would taunt them as cowards, and shouted that they did not *dare*. This was very trying to the piney-woods boys, who had always been brave and too venturesome for Mrs. Lee's comfort. It was not their mother, however, who had forbidden them to go out in the boat, but Grandma, who had seen too many people drown in the cruel water to be willing to trust her dear ones to the treacherous waves. She always watched with the keenest anxiety the frolicking boys in the boat.

Although Brer and Gene were not so familiar with the water as the shore boys, they were quite unwilling to be thought unequal to any sport, and least of all would they consent to being called cowards. It was too much of any one to expect of spirited boys to stand like girls on the wharf, and watch the fun without joining in.

Gene stood there in silence one day as long as he could bear it.

"*Mamma* never told us not to," he sputtered. "Grandma's always afraid we 'll drown if we wet our feet."

"No, Mamma never; she would n't either. She don't like to see us beat. I bet, if it were not for Grandma, she 'd tell us to go on and show those fellows what we can do," said Brer.

The boat came sweeping by just then before a driving gale.

"Hang your clothes on a hickory limb, but — " yelled one of the boys, waving his hand tauntingly.

"Just you come back for us," shouted Gene, angrily.

"We may as well go out once, just to show them," said Brer, rather uneasily. "If *Mamma* had told us not to, it would have been different, of course, but she never said a word."

"Yo' muder 's boun' be pow'ful mad w'en she year dose no' count boys callin' we-alls cowa'ds," said Nip, who was balancing himself on the wharf-railing.

"They won't have another chance," declared Gene. "Say, Brer, let 's hoist the mast in Grandma's boat, and show them what we can do."

"Grandma 's going to go for us just for going out with the other fellows. I reckon we 'd best leave her boat alone. Just see where those fellows are tacking to, will you? They 'll be out in deep water before they know it. Gee, how they rip along! They must be crazy going out that far!"

"'Pears lak dey-alls carn't pull de sail roun'," cried Nip, standing upright against the wind on the narrow wharf-railing, and gazing keenly at the flying boat.

"Looks like it, sure, or they 've lost their senses. No use in running out that far to get back here. I reckon I could show them something about tacking, if I *am* a land-lubber. Whew! Look at that, will you?"

The sail of the boat suddenly flew out, flapped madly from the mast an instant, and then dragged it down into the water. For one moment the watchers thought that the boat had gone down, but presently it rose from a trench upon a great swell, and they could see the four boys clinging to it.

"They 're all right," cried Brer, with a breath of relief. "I did n't know as they 'd find it so easy out there in deep water."

"Does yo' year dey-alls a-hollerin', Brer?" asked Nip, lifting his head to hearken.

"No. Do you?"

"I 'low I year right plain. Jes' a-w'oopin'. 'Pears lak deys gwine slip down de oder side de yerth, ef somebody doan tote dey-alls back."

"I really believe that they are drifting out. I bet they can't right the boat in that deep water. Look, Brer!" cried Gene.

But Brer had seen, and he was ready for action. "You Nip, get into that boat and bail her for all you 're worth. Gene, help me get the mast and sail from the bath-house!" were his prompt orders.

The boys had seen the mast set and the boat rigged for sailing many times; and though they never had actually managed her, they went to work under the pressure of excitement as if they were born sailors.

They had shoved the rocking boat from her moorings, and were getting well under way when Grandma, Mamma, and Aunty came running down the wharf, their hair blown by the wind and their dresses flapping about them.

"Mamma, we just have it to do," called Brer, appealing to his mother, before Grandma could say a word.

"They'll drown if we don't," screamed Gene.

The boys were mistaken in fearing Grandma's interference.   Though she strongly censured reckless and unnecessary exposure to danger, she was a wise, brave woman, encouraging bravery when there was real need for action.   She called to the boys quietly, for their mother was very pale and seemingly unable to speak.

"Be careful in shifting the sail.   When they're in, let Ross manage.   Tell him if he tips you out, I'll see that he is punished in a way that he will remember.   Will you do as I say?"

"Yes, sure!   Mamma, don't be scared."

It was no easy task to approach the upset boat in the teeth of the gale.   They were obliged to tack far out on this side and then

"And Brer and Gene each took an oar and managed to struggle alongside." — *Page* 277.

on the other, and so zigzag forward. How Brer managed, with his slight experience, to shift the sail without upsetting the boat, he never knew; but they kept right-side-up in spite of the buffeting wind and tossing water, and in a time really much shorter than it seemed to themselves or to those waiting and to those watching, they neared the capsized boat.

With the sail full of wind, scurrying along at breathless speed, it was impossible to come close to the other boat without danger of swamping it and of upsetting their own boat; so the three boys furled the sail as well as they could in such a tempest, and Brer and Gene each took an oar and managed to struggle alongside. The four exhausted boys scrambled aboard, and sank into the bottom of the boat.

Brer resigned the command to Ross, as Grandma had directed.

"She said how you are the best sailor, and

she said you are not to upset the boat again," he said briefly.

Ross flushed with shame.

"Your grandmother need n't be afraid I'll be up to any more tricks to-day. I've had enough water myself for once. I say, Brer," he went on awkwardly, "that was a right pretty show of tacking. I reckon I could n't have done better myself."

That was a right handsome concession from Ross, and Brer was more pleased by it than he cared to show.

"I'll tell you what," exclaimed one of the boys, when they had safely put about, unfurled the sail, and were speeding gayly toward the wharf. "We're bound to take back all we said about you-alls being cowards, ain't we, kids?"

"You bet!" was the hearty response; "and I say, Brer, you won't hear us calling you-alls 'land-lubbers' any more, either."

"Call ahead," said Brer, indifferently; "we don't care what names we go by."

"I care," cried Gene; "I ain't going to be called a coward by anybody."

"Doan yo' go fo' to upset de boat, Gene," cautioned Nip, sitting with all his small weight upon the upheaving side of the boat, "case Grammer's watchin' out from de w'arf, an' she boun' give yo' a pun'shment w'at yo' doan fo'git. W'oa, ole boat, w'at fo' yo' upsettin'?" he yelled, as the boat lurched against the wharf, and then coolly keeled over, as if that were the proper way to deliver its cargo, dumping them out into the shallow, seething water.

"We did n't go fo' to do it, Grammer," he sputtered, astride the keel in an instant. "Doan yo'-alls go fo' to fret yo'self. We-alls gwine set dis yer boat to rights befo' yo' done git de pone-cake from de safe fo' to soak up de wata from we-alls stomachs."

CHAPTER IX.

JOY'S MISHAPS.

"SEE mine! see my crab! it's the biggest of all!" screamed Joy, proudly swinging the great foolish fellow that was clinging so desperately to her line, as if it were clutching a life-preserver, instead of a death-bait.

"Great guns!" cried Gene, bending forward to see. "It is a fine one, sure. But what you fooling with it that-a-way for? Haul it up, quick! you'll lose it."

Joy began to pull in her line, and the row of children from all along shore, who were swinging their heels over the side of Grandma's wharf, and dangling long meat-baited strings into the water for the silly crabs to grab, watched the great clumsy pink creature rise dripping from the water and sway slowly up, up, up — splash !

" O-o-oh ! " screamed Joy and all the disappointed children in chorus.

" Oh, you-all hush ! " cried Brer, crossly, from the other side of the wharf, where he had dropped a half-dozen lines. " Have n't you got any sense ? You 'll scare off every blessed crab."

" Mine is n't scared off," said Joy. " Look, Nip, there he is, right on the bottom, see ? " Joy pushed back her little sun-bonnet, and leaned so far over the water that Nip, who was sitting beside her to bait her line, jumped up quickly and stood on her dress to prevent her falling. The water below was shallow, it is true; but the wharf was so high above it that a fall was not desirable. Nip could look down over Joy's head; he too saw the shining pink shell with the sunlight dancing over it.

" Let down yo' line, Joy, quick ! I reckon dat fool crab waitin' fo' noder bite."

"The bait's gone. The old thing done took it off," whimpered Joy.

"Doan go fo' to cry, honey. I's gwine tie some mo' meat on."

"Hurry!" whispered Joy, impatiently, thrusting the string into his hands, while she fixed the crab with the unwinking gaze of her two bright eyes.

"Let it down right easy," directed Nip, returning the string with a nice bit of fresh meat securely tied on the end.

Joy lowered the line with breathless caution. It touched the water, and ever so softly swept over the crab; but the old fellow never budged.

"He does just like he thought it nothing but a piece of seaweed," whispered Neal, too interested in Joy's crab to notice that another was pulling at her own line.

"Let the meat hit the old crab right hard," directed Gene.

Joy allowed the water to wash the meat

heavily backward and forward over the sprawling creature, but the crab took no heed except to move its claws a little uneasily.

"I 'low dat crab am feastin' on dat fust bait w'at he done grab, an' he doan wan' no mo'," said Nip.

"He 's got to take it!" cried Joy, ignoring, in her impatience, Brer's orders for quiet. "There, you old thing, catch hold, I say!" She made the meat dance about the crab until the water was stirred into little circling wavelets.

"Oh, quit that, Joy! You 'll scare him off, and all the rest too." Gene had just lost a bait.

" Jes' you hol' dat string right steady, Joy, an' bimeby dat ole crab gwine grab right tight," whispered Nip.

"No, he won't. He 's going now. Catch him! You Nip, catch him!"

" Carn't cotch 'im w'en he boun' to go," remonstrated Nip.

"Yes, you can too; jump right down and catch him! Hurry! he's going. Brer, make Nip catch him for me."

"I sha'n't do any such thing. Stop your row, can't you? How do you reckon he's going to catch him, — in his fingers?"

"He's going!" screamed Joy, who had kept her eyes on the precious crab. She scrambled to her feet and went pattering as fast as she could up the wharf to the sand.

"Wait, Joy, I's gwine cotch yo' fine crab fo' yo'," called Nip, as she gathered up her skirts and splashed out into the water.

"You're not going to do any such thing," cried Brer, peremptorily. "Let her lose her crab, now she's scared all ours away, and spoiled all our fun. You just stay where you are."

Joy waded straight toward the post near which she had seen the crab settle, recklessly ploughing the water up in front and carelessly trailing her skirts behind her. When she reached the spot, she was obliged to stand still a moment to let the disturbed water clear, and then — where was the crab?

"Why don't you catch him?" asked Brer, sarcastically.

"Pity to lose a crab that's worth all the others in the bay," remarked Gene, imitating his brother's tone.

"I 'low dat ole crab w'at yo' so fond ob—" began Nip, in the same strain — but what an interruption!

They had heard Joy scream many a time before, but this — who could have thought it possible for such a volume of screeches to be confined in her small body?

The children sprang to their feet and looked down upon her with terror.

Brer and Gene and Nip in a trice were off the wharf and beside the little sister.

In her distress she would have nothing to do with them.

The foolish child, in her determination to find the crab, had plunged her hand into the water to feel in the sand about the post.

" Ee — ee — ee ! " screaming with fright and pain, she jerked her hand from the water and shook it violently, but the strong claws of the crab, that had seized her, closed tighter and tighter, pinching her tender flesh most cruelly.

She turned upon the boys desperately, then back to the shore she plunged, and ran, screaming and howling at the top of her voice, toward Grandma's back gallery, while behind her streamed the boys and all the little playmates.

Neal's face was pale with alarm, and she too lifted up her voice in a series of shrieks; and all the little girls sniffed and sobbed in sympathy with poor little Joy.

What a hubbub! Mamma, Grandma, and Aunty came running out to meet them.

Mamma clasped the terrified child in her

"Screaming with fright and pain, she jerked her hand from the water
and shook it violently " — *Page* 286.

arms and frantically tried to loosen the stubborn claws. This was impossible to do, for the crab was as determined to keep Joy as Joy had been to keep it. Aunty ran for hot water into which to plunge the stubborn creature; but Brer meanwhile came to his mother's side, breathing hard, but speaking quietly, —

"Mamma, tell her to quit her yelling and hold her hand down there. I'll cut those nippers off."

"Joy, be brave, and do as your brother tells you."

Poor Joy stifled her cries, but quivered all over with pain and excitement, clinging to her mother, while Brer cut off the crab's claws.

What relief! All the little girls laughed and cried with her when she was free, and crowded around to examine the wounded hand, petting and kissing Joy "like she'd caught a potful of crabs for dinner, instead of driving them all out to sea, and scaring everybody out of their senses, because she done gone crazy over one pesky crab, and had stuck her fingers into its very claws," grumbled Brer, resenting the strain upon his feelings and the loss of the crabs he had planned to catch.

"We must remember that Joy is only a wee bit girlie," said Mamma, "and not expect her to be quite so brave as my big boys."

But that evening after tea, when she and Grandma and Aunty were sitting on the end of the wharf, enjoying the cool night breeze and the gorgeous reflections of the sunset on clouds and water, Mrs. Lee took occasion to reprove Joy for the foolish outcry which she had made over the crab.

Brer and Gene had pushed out in the boat to try their luck with the net; and there was no one to overhear Mamma's lecture but Neal, and Nip, who was lying on his stomach and propping his head in his hand, so that he might better watch the boys.

"Joy must remember when she is hurt that crying and screaming don't do one bit of good. It only makes the pain harder to bear; and it distresses other people."

"She screeched like an alligator had got her," exclaimed Neal, scornfully, quite forgetting how she had swelled the chorus, until Nip asked simply, —

"Did yo'-alls 'low a sha'k done kotch Joy, case why *yo'* yell so, Neal?"

"No, I did n't!" retorted Neal, glancing quickly at the teasing smiles of the three ladies. "I done thought it was a whale."

"Whales don't come to Grandma's Bay!" exclaimed Joy; "do they, Nip?"

"I 'low w'ales doan come, but sha'ks does, suah; case why, one snipped off de foot of a no 'count nigger dat carn't swim no mo' 'n a rock. I 'low Grammer's yern tell 'bout dat sha'k."

"Yes, Nip; but that was out beyond the Point. Sharks seldom come here."

"Say, Joy, suppose it had been a shark?" speculated Neal, opening her eyes wide as she imagined the great creature sweeping down on little Joy. "You'd have screeched then, I reckon."

"I reckon so," agreed Joy, cheerfully. The idea of anything more terrible than a crab was beyond her imagination.

"I 'low Joy ain't got no screech left big 'nough fo' a sha'k," grinned Nip.

"I have too! You just listen."

Joy stretched her mouth preparatory to showing her ability to salute a shark; but Mamma laid her hand softly over the yawning cavity.

"There, there, Joy. Wait until the shark comes. We've had enough screaming to-day. Listen! How softly the waves are lapping the shore! See the beautiful colors in the sky and the water."

"The bay looks just like a piece of the sky," said Neal. "See, the boys look just like they were floating in the clouds. They look just like they were cut out of black clouds; the boat, too, and their shadow, just as clear, upside down.

"Is n't it funny? Say, Nip, is that the way you and Flo and the man in the moon looked when you came a-sailing down to Grandma's Bay?"

"Dar ain't no fish a-floppin' up an' a-splashin' in de sky, Neal," expostulated Nip.

"Of course not. Only, just look, supposing the boat is the moon, and Brer — he's going to fall if he don't look out, throwing that net — and he was the man in the moon, and Gene (only you would n't be poling, like he is) was you, and you'd just come slipping down, as easy, through the rosy clouds. What makes the moon go, anyway?"

"I's gwine ax de man in de moon, bimeby," replied Nip, sleepily.

"Couldn't you see when you came, I'd like to know?"

"I's mostly sleepin' at night-time."

"Now, Nip, you weren't asleep when you were a-sailing in the moon."

"Nip never said he sailed in the moon," cried Joy.

"He never said he didn't; and how could he and Flo have come any other way?" argued Neal, who liked to believe in all sorts of wonderful things. "There's the moon-boat now?"

"Yes; the new moon again," observed Mrs. Lee. "We have been with Grandma and Aunty a whole long month. I reckon Papa and old Pacer will come for us in a few days. What do you say to that, boys?"

It had become quite dark except for the moon and stars and the phosphorescent glow on the water that broke like liquid fire against the posts of the wharf and the prow of the boat, which the boys, who had been coming slowly in, had tied to the landing.

"Home in a few days, — back to the Water-Oaks! How jolly!" shouted Gene. "Only —" he glanced around the enchanted moon-lit scene, at the sparkling water with the waving paths of moonlight and star-light lying across it, the lights of the city on the opposite shore, at the dear old villa on the cliff, with the dark, moss-hung oaks clustering about it, and the pines rising like gloomy giants behind it. Some one was singing far out over the water; and when the song was ended, and Aunty answered it in her sweet, low contralto, Gene slid down at her feet and hid his face among the soft folds of her dress, for it made him feel right homesick to think of leaving Grandma's Bay.

The children were greatly distracted between their desire to see the Water-Oaks again and their reluctance to leave the Bay. There was no immediate cause for distress, however, for Mr. Lee did not appear for nearly a week.

In that time Joy had an opportunity to show that she could be as plucky as any of them, now that she had made up her mind never again to be so babyish as she had been over that horrid crab.

It was late one afternoon, and the girls had just come up from their second daily plunge into the bay. Neal, in the room, was struggling into her shoes and stockings, and letting Mamma tie her into a ruffled white gown with pink ribbons, for it was the fashion on the Bay for all the girls to dress up and visit like little ladies every evening. Joy, lounging on the back gallery, waiting her turn to be dressed, was wondering what the boys were shouting and laughing about, down by the old store. She half

wished that she were a boy, then she would
not need to put on her shoes and stockings.
No, she did not wish that either, for boys
never wore such pretty dresses and ribbons,
and they always looked so funny and stiff
when they were dressed in their best suits.
Joy shook her brown head scornfully at the
thicket that hid the old store from sight.
"No, sir, I would n't be a boy if — Why,
Aunty!" She scrambled up the lattice for
a better view. Yes; it was Aunty who had
screamed. Joy could see her white dress
fluttering through the trees. And what was
that crashing through the bushes after her?
Oh, it was Mr. Jackson's pet deer, just tearing along!

Joy did not stop to consider. She jumped
from the gallery, and flying to the orchard
gate, pushed through, darted under the scuppernong arbor and under the orange-trees,
— no matter if something did prick her foot,
— and dashed with all her might against

the old gate that opened into the woods. Brush and briers were growing thickly against it, but she forced it open, and rushed out, tossing her arms and screaming, —

"Aunty! Aunty!"

Aunty saw her, and turned. The snorting deer was close behind her; but before his horns touched her, she swept little Joy back into the orchard, and pulled the gate close behind her.

Then, while the baffled deer tossed his cruel horns and stamped his sharp hoofs in baffled rage, Aunty sank down under the orange-trees.

"Oh, Aunty, don't!" cried Joy, terror-stricken by the white face and closing eyes. She stretched up her little arms for support as Aunty's head fell back heavily. Joy lowered it easily to the ground and flew back to the house, calling loudly for Grandma and Mamma.

She could not explain what was the matter with Aunty, but she seized Grandma's hand, and pulled her at an undignified pace to the orange orchard, Mamma and Neal following.

Grandma understood at a glance.

"She has fainted from fright," she said, kneeling by Aunty's side. "Send Joy for water, Lyla, and that bottle of scuppernong in the safe."

Mrs. Lee herself hastened to the house.

"Did the deer catch her? Is she dead?" whispered a horror-stricken voice at Grandma's side.

Brer and Gene and Nip, heading a troop of frightened boys, had come stealing into the orchard through a gap in the opposite fence.

Grandma turned upon the culprits sternly.

"Go straight away, boys! Have n't I told you hundreds of times not to aggravate that deer? Ross! Is Ross here? Go and tell your father to take his deer out of the woods, and to keep it out, or I shall have it shot. It has been a public nuisance long enough. Boys, I say to *go!*"

Never had Grandma addressed them in that tone before. The boys, filled with awful fear at the sight of Aunty's still face, slunk guiltily away.

Brer and Gene and Nip went slowly to the house.

Mamma came running down the steps.

"Is she dead?" gasped Gene, trying to clutch her skirts as she brushed by them; but Mamma only gave them a reproachful glance as she hurried on.

Brer led the way to the wharf, where they sank in a dejected row in the shade of the bath-house.

"Keep a watch-out on the house, Nip," commanded Brer, huskily.

This gave Nip some occupation. Brer and Gene kept their gaze turned carefully out to sea, thinking and thinking of Aunty's white face with the shadows of the orange-trees moving softly upon it, wondering if it still lay so, and wishing — oh, how they did wish — that they had let that deer alone.

After a time the silence became unendurable to Gene. His heart seemed swelled, and it ached so he could not stand it any longer. With a sob, he burst forth, —

"Oh, Brer, what shall we do? Let's not sit here; let's go back to the house."

"Grandma ordered us off," objected Brer, dully.

"But we can't sit here and think any longer; I shall just burst. If we've gone and made that deer kill Aunty, we're bound to do something."

"Do *what?* I'd like to know. Did n't Grandma tell us to go, like she never wanted to see us again? I'm sure I don't blame her."

"But let's *do* something."

"What *is* there to do, now she's dead?"

"Mamma wants us, I know," sobbed Gene. "I want to see Aunty again. I don't believe she's dead."

"Did n't you see her?" demanded Brer, huskily. Then he added, making a great effort to steady his voice,—

"You and Nip go. Go along with Gene, Nip."

Nip looked pleadingly at Brer.

"I 'low I's gwine 'bide yer wiv you, Brer," he coaxed.

"No; you go 'long with Gene," ordered Brer.

When he was alone, Brer buried his face in his arms and shook with sobs. He wept and moaned, his grief wrenching him sorely. Suddenly he controlled himself and sat up with a look of resolve on his pale face.

"I 'll go away," he muttered. "I 'll never show myself again to bother them. Gene is n't so old; and Nip — it does n't matter so much about them. But of course they all 'd hate the sight of me. Aunty — *she* would n't scold, but she — "

He ran rapidly down the steps and sprang into the dancing skiff. He never once looked at the house as he untied the boat and pushed off.

He rowed with all his might straight out into the bay. Where he was going he did not think. He did not think of anything but to get out of sight. Perhaps, in his dazed, grief-stricken mind, there was some vague idea of drifting out into the gulf, or perhaps of being picked up by some out-going steamer. It was not like Brer to act so impulsively, nor to take flight for any cause, but when had such a terrible thing happened! The very thought of it was too dreadful for endurance. He splashed wildly with his oars to drive the thought away. He would not even look up when a chorus of screams and shouts arose from the wharf. But though he refused to heed them, the cries confused him and hindered his movements. One oar slipped from his nerveless hand and floated away. It took much time to paddle after it and secure it.

The calls from the wharf became louder and more insistent.

"Brer! Brer! Come back!" That was Gene's voice. But now another cry sounded nearer, but faint.

"Brer! I's comin', Brer."

Brer started and lifted his head. What was that small round object bobbing along in the water?

"Brer!" again came the cry, more feebly.

Brer turned the boat and rowed rapidly back. Nip grasped the edge of the boat, but he was too exhausted to scramble in; Brer was obliged to help him.

"You Nip, what possessed you?"

"I reckon I was possess' by de sperit,

Brer," answered Nip, wiping his face on his sleeve.

"Do you want to slide off on the other side of the earth?" demanded Brer.

"I dunno. Is you gwine slide off, Brer?"

Brer slapped the water impatiently with the oars.

"Case why, Aunty gwine feel right bad, when yo'-alls doan come back right soon."

"Aunty!"

"Aunty 's done riz, Brer."

"Is she — is n't she dead?"

"Whar yo' eyes, Brer? Doan yo see Aunty a-standin' lak a sure 'nough ha'nt on de w'arf, a-screechin' an' a-wavin' to yo'-alls?"

Brer jumped upright in the boat and gazed back. There was Aunty indeed, standing on the very edge of the wharf, her tall white-clad figure gleaming in the last low rays of the sun, one hand shading her eyes and the other beckoning to him; and now he could hear her, for the others were still. "Brer! *oh-o-oh*, Brer!" How sweet and clear the prolonged notes sounded!

Brer made a trumpet with his hands and shouted back, "Coming; we're coming!"

What a long slow row that was back to the wharf! but Aunty stood there waiting for them as real as life. She had quite recovered from the fainting-fit too, or she never could have endured that *awful* hug that Brer gave her when he sprang up the steps.

"Why, Brer!" she exclaimed, laughing softly and running her white fingers through his hair; but she pretended not to see the tears in his eyes, which was just like Aunty.

"Hurry to your mother, Brer; she's worried about Joy. The poor child has got something in her foot. You'll have to run down to Point Myrtle, I reckon, and see if Dr. Beauregard came over in the steamer."

"A doctor! Joy must be badly off if Mamma could n't cure her."

Brer hastened to the house, expecting to find Joy in an alarming state. He was relieved to see her lying quietly on the couch with her foot in Grandma's lap.

The palm of the foot was badly swollen just back of the big toe; but the only sign of a wound was a tiny puncture like a pin-hole. "I fear it's an orange-thorn," said Mamma. "She said she felt a sting when she was running to open the gate for Aunty. She forgot all about it in the excitement, until I saw her limping."

"See if you can feel anything, Brer," said Joy, stretching out the little tanned foot.

Brer pressed his fingers upon the swollen flesh, until Joy snatched her foot back, laughing a little hysterically.

"It does n't hurt *much*," she said. "I don't want a doctor. Mamma 'll cure it."

"We 'll try a poultice to-night," decided Mamma; "to-morrow we will see about the doctor."

In the morning Joy was feverish and her foot much inflamed, so Mamma sent the boys for Dr. Beauregard.

He was a stout, jolly man, who laughed while he probed, and probed while he laughed, until Joy could have kicked him, if she had not been afraid of that sharp, glistening knife that hurt her enough as it was. Neal hid her face in Grandma's lap; but the boys, who saw Joy set her teeth in her determination not to scream, doubled their fists, that were tingling to show that great, heartless man what hurting was; while Nip, — that saucy little darky, — when he saw the doctor poising his lancet for another trial, gave the wrinkled skin of his fat neck such a tweak with his sharp fingers that Joy, who saw him, laughed, and it was the doctor who set his teeth, while he made a futile slap at the flea that he thought had bitten him.

He was so annoyed, being a city man, not so hardened to flea-bites as were over-the-

Bay people, that he forgot to probe any more.

He arose hastily, assuring Mamma positively there was not the least sign of any foreign substance in the foot,—a severe prick, nothing more; but he added pompously, —

"Keep it clean, Madam! keep it dry. The least carelessness or the least neglect is sure to bring on lockjaw. Take her away from the salt-sea air and the salt-sea water. Take her at once, Madam. Good-day."

He made a sweeping bow around the room, and puffed forth to his carriage.

"We'll send for my good old doctor to come by the steamer to-night," said Grandma; "we will run no risks."

"Is your doctor scared of fleas?" asked Joy.

"Not a bit; and he knows in a minute the difference between nipping fingers and biting fleas. I warn you, Nip."

There was no need to warn Nip. He

watched the grave, white-haired gentleman suspiciously at first; but when he saw how tenderly he handled Joy's poor inflamed foot, and how trustfully Joy smiled up at him, he concluded that this doctor did not need to be nipped, and he retired behind the boys, who were eying the doctor approvingly, for he produced no lancet from his case. He said to Mamma with a pleasant smile, "Only a little splinter, Lyla. It will work itself out. Just let it alone. This little girl will be jumping about like a cricket in a few days."

This good old doctor was mistaken, however. The foot grew worse; Joy became more feverish and fretful each day. Mrs. Lee began to think nervously of what the fat, pompous doctor had said about lockjaw.

How glad they all were, how relieved, when Papa at last came!

"We'll take her straight back into the piney woods," he decided at once. "She's bound to get well there. Can you be ready to start by four in the morning, Lyla?"

Mamma said "yes;" the children all cried "yes," and neither Grandma nor Aunty would say a word to detain them.

Accordingly, the next morning, while the night still lay black on the bay and the wavelets drowsily lapped the shore in the darkness, the sleepy children drank their strong coffee by the light of a kerosene lamp on Grandma's back gallery, and started on the long drive back into the piney woods, and before the scorching rays of the red sun had penetrated the open vistas of the pines, they were far on their way to the Water-Oaks.

Brer remained behind, not to ride up with the moon man, who doubtless would have refused accommodations to such a scoffer, but with Uncle Jim, who was promising himself a visit to the Water-Oaks within a few days.

Brer had resigned his seat in the wagon

to Nip, whom Joy, in a whimsical mood, had chosen for her nurse, and even for a day she refused to be separated from him.

Papa held his little girl in his strong arms while Pacer trotted bravely over the long, long road; and when, after a weary time of ceaseless jolting, the faithful old horse came to a standstill in the shade of the bay-tree, before the dear house gate, he carried her high above the welcoming cluster of barking, leaping dogs, and laid her tenderly upon a sheepskin pallet in the cool corner of the gallery.

Mamma bathed the throbbing foot with light, soothing touches, and skilfully bound it with strong sweet-gum salve of her own make.

Then Joy raised herself on her elbow and called imperatively, —

"Nip! Nip! You Nip!"

"Hi!" came the prompt response from the old orchard, where Gene and Nip were scrambling over the roof of the scuppernong arbor, taking an inventory of the grape crop, popping the occasional ripe grapes that their searching eyes discovered into their ready mouths, and dropping some into the greedy apron that Neal held stretched to its most gaping width beneath them.

Nip swung himself down by the great scuppernong trunk that supported the centre of the arbor, and sped lightly to the gallery where Joy continued her petulant calling, —

"Nip! Nip! You Nip!"

"Yer I is, Joy. W'at fo' yo' yellin' lak I 's down yonda at Grammer's Bay? Doan go fo' to 'cite yo'self fo' not'in' an' mek yo'self right feberish," remonstrated Nip, pattering along the gallery and dropping down at Joy's side with an offering of four great luscious grapes in his extended hand. "I 'low yo' doan wan' dese yer fine ripe grapes."

"Yes, I do," declared Joy, sitting up and

taking three grapes. "Now, you eat that one right slow for company," she said, pushing away his hand with the other grape in it.

Nip obediently munched his grape in sociable leisure until Joy's grapes had disappeared and she issued her next order, —

"Tell them to bring us some more."

"Hi, dar!" yelled Nip, springing to his feet and facing the scuppernong arbor. "Doan yo' go fo' to roll all dose fine scuppernongs down yo'-alls frote. Case why, Joy 'low she gwine war yo'-alls out ef Neal doan fotch her an apernful ob grapes right soon. D' year?"

"Now conjure it," was Joy's next command, as she sank back and stretched out her bandaged foot.

"All right, honey. Mind yo' 'bide right still. Nip gwine conjure dat ole splinter so he boun' show hisself."

The little darky dropped on his knees

and made a strange sign over the injured foot. Then, working his face into fascinating contortions, rolling up his eyes in awful solemnity, and moving his lips in indistinct mutterings, he waved his slender brown hands in circles and other mystic signs over the throbbing wound; while Joy watched him with a breathless interest that was partly amusement, but more than half superstitious belief.

"Now dat ar foot gwine git well right sma't," declared Nip, when the spell was completed. "Doan go fo' to fret yo'self any mo' 'bout dat splinter. Dat splinter am comin' out."

Of course Nip was right.

Two mornings after, on the day of Brer's arrival with Uncle Jim, when Mamma was dressing the foot, she discovered a speck in the swollen flesh. She tried in various ways to remove it, but all her attempts being unsuccessful, she at last called Papa.

Mr. Lee examined the spot carefully, and then sent Brer for the pincers.

"I'm going to hurt you some, Joy," he said; "but if you will sit right still in Mamma's lap and stand the pain like a brave little woman, it will be over in a minute, and in a few days we'll have a well foot. Besides," said Papa, mysteriously, "when this splinter is out, I'm going to tell you a secret."

"What, Papa?" cried Neal, with widening eyes.

"Never mind. I'm going to tell Joy first, and she can tell the rest of you. Now be brave, little girl."

Joy clung close in Mamma's helpful arms, not uttering a cry until all was over, then she could not help sobbing a little from pain and excitement. In a minute she sat up, and laughing hysterically, brushed away the tears to see the splinter that the boys were exclaiming over.

It was an orange-thorn, fully an inch in length, that had been buried in Joy's small foot, hiding from the two wise doctors as well as from everybody else.

"Gee!" cried Brer, with mock concern. "I should hate to have Joy step on me. I say, Mamma, I wish you'd make her wear shoes. It's right dangerous to have her round here barefoot. Suppose, now, she should step on one of us, where would we be?"

"Ger-ate guns!" cried Gene. "I never thought of that. We'd be worse off than Joner in the whale, once we got caught in Joy's foot."

"I reckon Nip's fingers or Mamma's salve could conjure you out," laughed Papa, as he went down the steps. The determined clutch of a small hand stopped him.

"Well, daughter, what is it?" he asked, looking down into Neal's shining eyes.

"The secret," she demanded.

"Sure, I forgot." He returned to Mamma's side, and bending down, whispered very softly in Joy's ear.

Joy's face flushed and her eyes snapped as she listened.

"*You* don't know," she cried, clapping her hands and laughing roguishly at the eager faces about her.

"Papa said for you to tell," screamed Neal, stepping on Mamma's toe in her excitement.

"Well," began Joy, promisingly. Then she paused and pursed her lips. "It's a secret," she declared, shaking her head.

"Now, you tell!" demanded Gene.

"A new —" Joy looked up at Mamma and laughed. "A new —" again she paused tantalizingly.

"Oh, don't tell unless you want to. I reckon it isn't worth telling," said Brer, turning his back.

"It is too! A new teacher is coming! — and Tommy!"

"Tommy!"

"Who?"

"When?"

"Where from?"

"Tommy?"

"Who's Tommy?"

"Tommy is a little Yankee boy, coming down to the Water-Oaks with his cousin who is going to live in the Owlets' Roost this winter and teach you boys."

Mamma's explanation was followed by a pause of dubious silence. The introduction of a little stranger among them was a matter of serious importance to the children.

"Is Tommy going to school?" asked Neal, at last.

"Yes."

"We'll have Nip!" cried Joy, triumphantly.

"How do you know you'll have Nip? Come along, you Nip." Gene cast a look of defiance at the girls, and with Nip in his

wake, followed Brer out to the new barn
to talk the unexpected news over. The
boys betook themselves to the corn-crib, and
husked numberless ears of corn on the subject, but at last they could not quite make
up their minds about Tommy.

"I should n't mind seeing a Yankee boy,"
grumbled Gene; "but somehow Tommy —
Tommy sounds like a period."

"A period?" demanded Brer.

"Like a stop to things, you see. It 'll
be different with him around."

"Of course it won't be like having it all
to ourselves," agreed Brer.

"Tommy sha'n't come to the Water-
Oaks," declared Gene, with sudden heat.

"Oh, come now, Gene, what 's the use?
We 're bound to have him. I reckon he 'll
be a heap of fun too. Papa says Yankees
are up to all sorts of things, you know.
I wonder what he 's like." So they fell
to speculating about the little stranger.

Gene's instinctive feeling that Tommy's advent to the piney woods would end the first volume of their happy, lonely times, was natural and true to the event; but Brer also was right in anticipating the coming of the little Yankee from away up yonder as the beginning of a new chapter in their lives of fresh and lively interest.

THE END.